The Little Things

THE LITTLE THINGS

M. JEAN PIKE

THORNDIKE PRESS
A part of Gale, a Cengage Company

Copyright © 2023 by M. Jean Pike.
All scripture quotations, unless otherwise indicated, are taken from the Holy Bible, New International Version®, NIV®, Copyright 1973, 1978, 1984, 2011 by Biblica, Inc.™ Used by permission of Zondervan. All rights reserved worldwide. www.zondervan.com
Scripture quotations marked KJV are taken from the King James translation, public domain. Scripture quotations marked DR, are taken from the Douay Rheims translation, public domain.
Scripture texts marked NAB are taken from the *New American Bible, revised edition* Copyright 2010, 1991, 1986, 1970 Confraternity of Christian Doctrine, Washington, D.C. and are used by permission of the copyright owner. All Rights Reserved. No part of the New American Bible may be reproduced in any form without permission in writing from the copyright owner.
Thorndike Press, a part of Gale, a Cengage Company.

ALL RIGHTS RESERVED
This is a work of fiction. Names, characters, places, and incidents either are the product of the author's imagination or are used fictitiously, and any resemblance to actual persons living or dead, business establishments, events, or locales, is entirely coincidental.
Thorndike Press® Large Print Christian Romance.
The text of this Large Print edition is unabridged.
Other aspects of the book may vary from the original edition.
Set in 16 pt. Plantin.

**LIBRARY OF CONGRESS CIP DATA ON FILE.
CATALOGUING IN PUBLICATION FOR THIS BOOK
IS AVAILABLE FROM THE LIBRARY OF CONGRESS.**

ISBN-13: 979-8-88579-629-3 (hardcover alk. paper)

Published in 2024 by arrangement with White Rose Publishing, a division of Pelican Ventures LLC.

Printed in Mexico
Printed Number: 1   Print Year: 2024

For Sue S, my sister in Christ, who helped me find my way. And for Doreen J, whose door was always open and the coffee, always on. The little things meant so much!

1

Rochelle could've cried over the condition of Bessie's flower beds. By mid-April, the daffodils and the Rembrandt tulips should have been in peak bloom, a dazzling display of red and gold that made people drive around the block for a second look. Now they were suffocating under years' worth of decaying leaves and crab grass.

The house hadn't fared any better. Crumbling bricks flanked the wide front steps and came to rest on tottering porch spindles, leaning against each other like drunken soldiers. Nine years had taken its toll, in more ways than one.

"The HVAC is acting up," Austin said, coaxing a key into the lock. "But if the weather holds, you should be fine here for a couple of weeks."

"A couple of weeks?"

"You didn't mention your plans, but I'm sure you won't want to stay longer than that. Glamorous California obviously has a greater pull than Ohio and your family."

She hadn't planned anything beyond today and the sanctuary of her beloved Bessie's home.

"Actually, I can't imagine why you'd choose to return now."

She glanced at her brother and saw a hundred unspoken words in his expression. Saw what had seethed just beneath the surface of their awkward hug at the bus station and filled the uncomfortable silence ever since.

After a few moments of persuasion, the key turned, the door groaned open, and she followed him inside. The air smelled like mildew and sickness, accentuated by the murky darkness. An aged bulldog sat in the kitchen doorway. His cloudy eyes looked past them expectantly. Seeing no one else, he turned and slunk back to the kitchen.

"That's Gus," Austin said. "He'll need some taking care of."

"Is he wearing a diaper?"

"He has bladder issues. There's a bag of pads on the table. You'll need to change him every few hours."

Great. "I didn't know Bessie had a dog."

He shot her a furious glance. Her baby

brother would never forgive her for going away.

"We got him for her when she first got diagnosed. Kat read an article about how dogs promote health and wellness, or some such thing." He shrugged. "It was worth a try."

Rochelle flipped the switch beside the door. Dim light pooled into the room, accompanied by the clatter of the ceiling fan. A dark stain spread from its center. She moved past her brother and tugged on the window until it grudgingly opened and filled her lungs with cool, fresh air. The back garden was unkempt, the gutter on Bessie's garden shed flapped in the breeze. A pair of black rubber boots waited patiently in the weeds beside the door.

I had an appointment last week. They tell me the cancer's back, but don't you worry about it, darling girl. One way or another I'll be just fine. God will be by my side, just as He's always been . . .

The sadness was more than Rochelle could bear, and tears clogged her throat. She turned to face her brother. "Thanks for picking me up."

"No problem. Do you need anything before I go?"

"Does the dog have plenty of food?"

"There should be a bag on the table. Kat was here this morning, so he's all set for today. He hasn't been eating much lately."

She moved to the kitchen, picked up the bag of dog food, and shook it. Almost half full. Gus looked at her hopefully, so she refilled his dish. Retrieving his water bowl, she carried it to the sink. When she turned on the tap, the faucet escaped its fitting and crashed into the sink. An icy blast of water shot out, spraying her face and sopping the front of her shirt.

"Good grief!" She turned off the tap and groped for the red-checkered dish towel beside the sink. As she swiped at her hair and face, the emotions she could no longer suppress came pouring out. The sadness, the fear, and the overwhelming stress of the past six days. "This place is falling apart, Austin. How did it get like this?"

"Do you really want to go there with me, Rochelle?"

His tone caused her to look up. He was deadly calm on the outside, but clearly furious within.

No, no, no! This wasn't the way she meant for it to go, all of this anger and bitterness. Not when so much time had already been lost.

When he'd picked her up at the bus station, she'd barely recognized him. She'd left home at twenty-one, when he was just a boy of sixteen. Today he stood before her, a man of twenty-five. So handsome in his suit and tie, so capable, her baby brother, a police detective, a husband, and soon to be a father. He was angry with her for going away, but it wasn't a crime to want more than a life of potluck suppers and Friday night football games. More than what the small town of Redford's Crossing had to offer. She'd meant to sit down with him over a cup of coffee and explain it to him. She hadn't meant for it to go like this at all.

"Look, I didn't mean —"

"Who do you think pumped out the cellar the last time it rained? Who do you think patched the roof and cut the lawn and took the dog to the vet? Who do you think took Bessie to the grocery store, the doctor's appointments, and the beauty shop for the past two years when she wasn't able to drive anymore? All that on top of keeping up my own house while putting in almost sixty hours a week at the station. So you'll have to excuse me if this place isn't quite up to your standards."

"Austin, I'm sorry."

But he wasn't finished. He'd barely begun.

"And when she got too sick to stay here

alone," he roared, "it was my wife, my *pregnant* wife, who came over every single day and took care of *your* foster mother while you were living it up out there in la-la land!"

His words crashed against her like a slap across the face. They were excruciating. They stole her breath. "It wasn't like that. It wasn't some glamorous life. It was . . . a hard life."

"If it was so hard then why didn't you come home?"

"It . . ." Her voice broke. "It wasn't that easy."

"Yeah, it never is with you, is it?"

Gus growled low in his throat.

A quiet cough from behind made them both turn.

A man stood in the kitchen doorway, a very large man, his broad shoulders filling the entire space. He wore a faded, blue denim shirt, and a pair of well-worn jeans, a working man's clothes. His hair was close cropped and blond, tidy except for an unruly cowlick in the front and even in the dim light Rochelle could see that his eyes were a startling shade of blue.

"I saw the car in the driveway," he said. "Is this a bad time?"

Austin recovered quickly. "Oh, hey, Sandy. No, not at all. I'm on my way back to the station, but my sister will be here. Go ahead and look around. I'll give you a call later."

Look around?

He moved aside.

Austin slid past him and disappeared. When the front door thudded closed behind him, Ro turned her gaze back to the man. "I'm sorry you had to witness that."

He lifted his shoulder in a shrug. "I know how it is. I have a brother."

He stood there, staring at her, as if he were waiting for something. Finally, he said, "You're Rochelle, right?"

She searched his face, clearly at a disadvantage. "Yes."

"Sandy Fairbrother. Maybe you don't remember me."

She vaguely remembered the name. Her gaze moved over him, her mind trying to reconcile this big, handsome man with the thin, quiet boy she barely remembered from high school. Nice enough looking, but not gorgeous. Athletic enough to be on the sports teams, football, she thought, but not first string. Just an average boy. "Of course," she said.

"So, you're back."

"The prodigal daughter returns."

"I'm sorry for your loss. Bess was a wonderful woman."

"Thank you." An awkward moment of silence passed. "May I ask what you're doing here?"

"Austin mentioned that he assumed Bess left the house to the two of you in her will. He said he was hoping to unload it quickly and wondered if I'd be interested in buying it."

The shock of his words was like second slap. No, more like a throat punch. "Why would you be?"

"I own a few rental properties around town, as well as a small construction company. I do renovations, buy and flip homes, that sort of thing. I told Austin I'd be happy to take a look at the place."

His words spun around inside her head, making her dizzy. The one place in the world where she felt safe was in danger of being sold? Torn away from her? Fear slithered inside her stomach and rose up the back of her throat as her last hope of security slipped away. *Oh, Lord. Don't let me be sick.* Pulling in a breath to calm herself, she tossed the checkered dishcloth into the sink. "Austin really should have discussed this with me first, before talking to you. We haven't made any definite plans for the house yet."

"Right. Well, I just thought —"

"You thought what?" She fixed him with an angry stare. "My foster mother is barely laid to rest, and you come swooping in here to take advantage of us for the opportunity to feather your own nest?"

He seemed momentarily taken aback. Then he grinned, infuriating her farther. "I wouldn't exactly say I swooped. I walked in through the front door. *After* your brother invited me."

"Well I'm sorry you've wasted your time. Until further notice, this house is not for sale. Understood?"

He watched her for a long moment, something unreadable in his expression. Amusement, definitely, but something else as well.

"Understood."

It took all the self-control Sandy had not to stalk back to his truck. In case she was watching from the window, he attempted a swagger. He slid behind the wheel, turned the key, and drove away, hoping he appeared calmer than he felt. What on earth was her problem? And for that matter, what was his?

She was tiny, maybe a hundred and twenty pounds soaking wet, which at the moment she was, but she still had the power to make him feel small.

No, not small. Insignificant.

15

Then why didn't you come home?
It wasn't that easy . . .

Maybe she was annoyed that he'd overheard. He hadn't meant to eavesdrop on her conversation with Austin. He should have called ahead and set up an appointment to look at the house, but word traveled pretty fast around town that Rochelle Delany was coming back to Redford's Crossing to help settle Bess' house and estate. If he were honest, he'd admit he'd stopped by unannounced hoping to catch a glimpse of her.

Which had worked out just fabulously.

Still, Austin's question was one that had been on the lips of half the town. Why hadn't Rochelle come home before now? Nearly a decade of Christmases, homecomings, and other special occasions had come and gone with no sign of her. When Bess' cancer returned, people thought surely Rochelle would come home, take care of her, as she had before.

Sandy frowned. She hadn't even been there for the funeral. Bess didn't deserve that, after all she'd done for Rochelle and Austin. Was her life in California that all fired important and glamorous that she couldn't tear herself away a few days earlier to say goodbye to the woman who'd raised her?

Rochelle was still beautiful — as lovely a woman as she'd been a girl. Still every bit as exotic, with her long black hair, her dark eyes, and those full, red lips. She still stole his breath away, just as she had in high school. But somehow, the sparkle was gone from those beautiful brown eyes. She seemed weary, as if life had used her up.

Still full of fight, though, obviously.

Two short honks shattered his thoughts, and he moved through the green light with an apologetic wave to Mary Maxwell in the burgundy sedan behind him.

Rochelle Delany, after all these years.

What was her reason for wanting to hold onto the house? He would have loved to buy the solid little craftsman on Orchard Drive. With some work, it could be renovated and flipped and he could make a nice profit. Austin had made it sound as if Sandy would be doing them a favor to take it, so what was the problem? Why had Rochelle marched him out the door like that? Surely, she wasn't planning to keep it, to move back to Redford's Crossing permanently, and live in it. His heartbeat quickened at the thought. She'd been gone for such a long time. He'd missed her more than he had any reason to, except . . .

He was sure she didn't even remember the kiss. It was an insane, impulsive moment that meant nothing to a popular cheerleader. But to a lonely boy, it meant everything. It was his first kiss, and he'd never forgotten it.

Later that evening, Rochelle was ashamed of the way she'd acted. She'd been humiliated to discover someone had overheard Austin's accusations and had reacted in anger. Sandy Fairbrother seemed like a decent man, and he'd seemed genuinely happy to see her. It wasn't his fault her foolish choices had left her in this precarious position. Nor was it Austin's. Her brother had probably assumed she would be glad he'd taken the initiative in selling the house, assumed she'd be anxious to head back to California. He had no way of knowing how wrong he was.

She sighed. "What will become of us, Gus?"

The dog lifted his head and regarded her for a long moment, then plodded to the back door and scratched at it.

"Do you need to go out?"

He frowned at her, as if to say, *"Obviously."*

She removed his diaper, dumped it in the

trash bin, and led him out to the backyard. There was a chill in the evening air, and she clutched her sweater close as she stood looking at the only house she'd ever considered home. She was ten, and Austin, only five, when their parents drove away from their broken-down trailer on the outskirts of town and never came back. Ravaged by a recent battle with cancer, Bessie agreed to take them in for a week or two until Social Services could sort it all out.

They never left.

In Bessie's home and in her incredible heart Rochelle had found comfort, a place where she belonged, but being abandoned left its scars. She became a perfectionist, pushing herself to excel at everything she did. Second place was not an option. You were the best, or you were nothing at all. She decided early on that she would be the queen of the homecoming dance. The queen of the prom. She would be the queen of everything. And she would never feel unwanted again. She had the drive to succeed and the need to feel important. Those things led to her desperate situation in California. And now she was probably on Menzo's hit list. Was two thousand miles far enough away to be safe?

A quiet snort came from the door. Gus

was finished with his business and waited to go back inside. In the kitchen, she retrieved a doggie diaper from the bag and studied it from every angle until it made sense.

"OK, boy. Let's do this."

Her first attempt at diapering Gus was a disaster. The second was only slightly better, baggy and lopsided, but at least everything important was covered. When she'd fastened the tabs, she patted his head. "Thanks for being patient with me. That looks pretty good, don't you think?"

He chuffed his agreement and wandered back to his ratty, red-plaid pillow in the corner. As she bent and patted him, a wave of lightheadedness nearly knocked her over. She'd barely eaten in a week, and not at all today. Standing, she drew a breath to steady herself and then moved to the cupboard to investigate. Maybe she could find some crackers, or a can of soup.

It was then that she noticed the paper sack beside the toaster, a note propped against it.

    Rochelle,
    Welcome home! I didn't figure you'd want to go to the store after being on the road all day, so I picked up a few things to get you started. I can't wait to finally meet

you! Let's get together soon! Call us if you need anything.

Kat

The bag contained a can of coffee, a package of bagels, a jar of peanut butter, and one of strawberry jelly. Though she was grateful, Kat's thoughtfulness filled Rochelle with guilt. She'd missed her brother's wedding, had never even met his wife.

Kat's the sweetest little thing you can imagine, Bessie had written her. *But just as fiery as her red hair when she gets a notion in her head. I just know you'll love her. Please say you're able to come for the wedding . . .*

She blinked back the tears that never seemed to stop any more. When Rochelle left for California, Bessie had been well, tending her gardens, singing in the church choir, volunteering in the literacy program at the library. Over the years, her letters had been filled with tidbits of Redford's Crossing gossip and news of her flower beds and what was currently in bloom. And always, always, a request for Rochelle to come home.

Can you come for your birthday next month, darling? I can help out with your plane ticket, if it's that. I'll make sausage lasagna for your homecoming, and your favorite German Choc-

olate cake . . .

The tears spilled over and slid, unchecked, down her face as she imagined how hurt Bessie must have been when she didn't come home. She must have thought Rochelle didn't care about her, didn't love her anymore. Nothing could have been further from the truth.

"I'm so sorry, Bessie," she whispered. "I'd have given anything to be here with you. To be even half the woman you were . . ."

In her teenage arrogance, Rochelle had thought she had it all figured out. Her plan was to go to college, and then get a fabulous career and make piles of money. With Bessie's careful spending, and her God-will-provide faith, they'd made it through many hard times. But sometimes just barely.

Ask and you shall receive, Bessie liked to say. And she had asked. When the car needed repairs or the roof began to leak. God always provided what Bessie asked for. But in Rochelle's estimation, Bessie hadn't asked for enough.

A sudden, sharp knocking at the front door exploded in the quiet like a gunshot.

Rochelle froze.

Who could that be? No one except her brother and Sandy Fairbrother knew she was in town. Menzo couldn't possibly have tracked her down already, could he?

"Rochelle! Are you in there?" a man's voice boomed. It didn't sound like Sandy, and it definitely wasn't Austin. One of Menzo's thugs?

She sat rooted to the chair, her pulse roaring in her ears and her stomach clenched in terror.

2

Gus growled, a low, menacing rumble deep in his throat.

"Shhh, it's OK, boy," Rochelle whispered. But she wasn't at all sure that it was.

The knock came again.

Gus barked and plodded to the foyer to investigate. As he sniffed at the crack beneath the front door, Rochelle stood on shaking legs and crept toward the window. She was considering whether to chance a peek outside.

"Rochelle, it's Jan and Russ Swanson from next door. Remember us?" a woman said.

Ro blew out a breath. *Thank you, God.* Composing herself, she pasted on a smile and opened the door. "Mr. and Mrs. Swanson, hello! How nice to see you both again."

Jan Swanson's face was older than Ro remembered and deeply creased with wrinkles, but at that moment, it seemed like the most beautiful face she had ever seen.

"We saw you earlier with Austin, so I made up a pot pie for your dinner. I'm sure you've had a long day, so we won't stay but a minute." She extended a steaming dish. "Welcome home."

"Thank you very much." Ro took the dish from Jan's hands, nearly swooning from the savory aromas of chicken and vegetables. "That's really sweet of you."

"We were mighty sorry to hear about Bessie's passing," Russ said. "She was a wonderful neighbor, and she'll be greatly missed."

"Thank you."

"It's nice to have you home, Rochelle," Jan said. "I look back so fondly on those years of watching you and Austin growing up. I just don't know where the years have gotten to. Will you be staying in Redford's Crossing for a while?"

"I don't really have any definite plans."

"We'd like to have you over for dinner one of these nights. Get caught up, as they say. You just let us know when it's convenient."

"I'd like that."

"I'm sure you have plenty of work ahead of you, sorting through Bessie's things and all." Russ' gaze moved past her and into the house.

"Yes, that's for sure."

"I'd love to have a little something to remember her by," Jan said wistfully. "If you should come across a pretty tea cup, while you're sorting, or a little figurine. Anything at all, really."

"I'll be sure to keep that in mind, Mrs. Swanson."

"Well, you just let us know if you need anything, honey. We're always home."

When they left, Ro carried the pot pie to the kitchen and cut a thick slice. The chicken and vegetables melted in her mouth, as she'd known they would. Jan Swanson had always been a wonderful cook and a wonderful neighbor. The Swansons were always the first to step in and lend a hand.

Living in a small community had always been a two-sided coin. There was no such thing as privacy in Redford's Crossing. Friends' and neighbors' secrets were passed across the tables at the Top of the Town diner like bottomless cups of coffee. There was a certain amount of intimacy in living among folks you'd known all your life. A connectedness you didn't get in a big city. As a restless teenager, though, Ro hadn't felt connected. She'd felt smothered. Bored with Redford Crossing's five blocks of Main Street, with its movie theater and its bowling alley. Nothing ever seemed to change here, and she was desperate to escape the dull predictability of small-town life.

The summer Ro graduated from high school, Bessie's cancer came back and leaving was out of the question. She took a part-time job as a cashier at Wally's Corner Market and devoted the rest of her time to taking care of Bessie and Austin. After six months of careful saving, hungry for anything that seemed like an adventure, she blew her entire bank account on an expensive computer, the first bad choice in a long string of bad choices that would ultimately destroy her life.

When Ro had finished a second helping of pot pie, she took a long, hot shower and changed into one of Bessie's old nightgowns, then wandered to her old bedroom and climbed into bed, overtaken with exhaustion. But lying in the dark, her fears crept in again. Every sound, every sweep of the headlights across the wall seemed like approaching danger. The Swansons were right next door, but they were close to eighty years old. If there were any sort of commotion in the night, would they even hear it?

"Gus?" she called softly.

Nails clicked on the hardwood floor, and Gus' grumpy face appeared in the doorway.

"Hey, would you mind sleeping in here with me tonight?" She patted the spot at the foot of the bed. He regarded her from the doorway, his bulldog mouth dipped down in a frown.

"Please?"

Finally, he chuffed his consent and plodded toward her. She got out of bed and hefted him up.

"Oh, my goodness, you're a tank, you know that? We'll have to see about getting you some exercise. Do you like to walk?"

Ignoring the question, he pawed at the blankets, then circled twice and plopped down at the foot of the bed.

"You'll let me know if you hear anything, right?" she asked. "Like, if you hear anyone trying to get in the house? That's what dogs do, isn't it?"

He heaved a longsuffering sigh.

Rochelle stared at the ceiling, reviewing the day and how her thoughtless remarks had added to Austin's anger. And Sandy Fairbrother, with his easy smile and his amazing blue eyes, she'd made him angry, too. She wished she could start the day over.

Lying in the dark, she was visited by vague memories of Sandy coming into the store when she was working, to buy a drink or a candy bar. He made awkward small talk with her while she rang up his purchases. It seemed to her now that he'd always been on the periphery of her life. Why had she never paid attention to him?

Because he hadn't been nearly as good looking then as he was now. How shallow she'd been.

In any case, selling him the house was out of the question. She thought she'd have a few days to think of a way to present her plan to Austin, to talk things over with him. She certainly hadn't known she'd have to fight off a prospective buyer the moment she got home.

Home.

Could she really slide back into her life in Redford's Crossing, reclaim her home and her relationship with her brother? Could she eventually find work, buy Austin out and own Bessie's house outright? She had so many questions, but no solid answers. One thing was for sure. She would never go back to Sunny Springs, California. Best case scenario, Menzo would have her arrested. Worst case, he'd have her killed.

3

The next morning as he drove through town, Sandy was only half listening to the nonstop flow of chatter from the backseat. It had been a long, sleepless night and he was having trouble focusing.

"Daddy, after the board store, can we get a milkshake?"

Sandy shot a glance at his son in the rearview mirror and pretended to think about the request, as though he hadn't had the very same thing in mind. "You think we should, do you?"

"Yes, yes!" Jace bounced up and down in his booster seat.

"I suppose we can do that. We probably better get a burger to go with it, too. It's almost lunch time already."

"That's 'cause it took *sooo* long at the tool store."

Sandy hid a smile. Five days a week just weren't enough to keep up with the demands of his growing business, so more often than not, he and Jace spent Saturdays at the salvage depot, or the lumber yard, or the hardware store, negotiating for the best deals Sandy could get on materials for his current renovation project. Jace took the jaunts like a trooper, and Sandy always tried to inject a little bit of fun into the day. Most times, that meant burgers and shakes at Maddy's Diner.

"Are you starving?"

"Uh-huh."

"Maybe we'd better skip the board store for today then, you think?"

"OK!" The boy was bouncing like a basketball now, most likely already tasting the creamy deliciousness of one of Maddy Sheridan's strawberry milkshakes. "And Dad, after the milkshakes can we go to the plaza?"

Sandy affected a look of horror. "The plaza?"

Jace grinned. "Yeah. Dakota got this really cool action figure. I want to get one, too."

"*Action figure!* What do you think, I'm made of money?"

The impish face erupted in giggles. "No! You're made of bones and skin, just like me!"

"Action figure, indeed."

31

But he would buy whatever new toy Jace had in mind. His son asked for very little, and there was nothing Sandy would deny him.

When they pulled into Maddy's Diner at a quarter to noon, the parking lot was nearly empty. Two years before, a strip mall had been built in an abandoned field outside of town. What seemed overnight, popular stores and restaurants shot up like jimsonweed and choked out several of the town's mom 'n' pop businesses. There were clothing stores and shoe stores, craft outlets and jewelry boutiques. There were restaurants offering a wide-screen TV on every wall and dishes prepared with ingredients he couldn't pronounce. Sandy preferred Maddy's, with its slightly tacky décor and stick-to-your-ribs comfort foods. Namely, the thickest, juiciest burgers in Jasper County.

Once inside, Jace sprinted to their regular booth and claimed his spot beside the window.

"Hey, handsome," the owner, Madeline Sheridan, called out as Sandy walked in.

"Hello, Maddy."

"And who's this young man?" she asked, setting a plastic placemat and a roll of silverware in front of Jace.

Jace giggled. "It's me, Jacey."

"Oh, it couldn't be. Mercy sakes, you're shooting up like a little bean stalk, aren't you? Soon you'll be taller than me."

It wasn't saying much. In her late sixties, Maddy was already stooped with osteoporosis. And though her hands were knotted with arthritis, she still insisted on preparing most of the diner's food herself.

"I'm seven already!" Jace gleefully informed her.

"Seven years old," She made a clicking sound with her tongue. "I remember when you were born. Seems like yesterday. Getting your usual?"

"Two burgers, two orders of French fries, and two strawberry milkshakes," Sandy said. "And a coffee. Black."

"What, no coffee for your partner?"

"Noo!" Jace shouted. "I don't like coffee!"

Maddy chuckled and turned her attention back to Sandy. "Carol-Anne was just talking about you this morning."

Sandy's stomach clenched. Why wasn't he surprised?

"Was she?"

"That light on her front porch blew out again. I wish you'd stop by and take a look at it. What with her shifts at the hospital, coming and going late at night. Well, a single woman can't be too careful."

Carol-Anne Sheridan stressed him out to no end. She'd moved into one of his rentals the year before and had been inventing reasons for him to stop by ever since. She was always pointing out that she was a single girl, living alone. His lips turned down in a frown. Carol-Anne was in little danger on Parkview Drive, considering the police station was right around the corner.

"I'll have Judge stop by and take another look at it this week."

"I know you're busy, hon, but I really wish you'd go yourself. Judge obviously didn't fix it right the last time."

Maddy's transparent ploy on behalf of her daughter was ruining his appetite. At thirty and divorced, with a thriving construction business and eleven rental homes to his name, some of the single ladies around town had him on their list of eligible prospects. Carol-Anne made it no secret that she would love to be the one to remove him from that list. But Sandy wasn't looking for a wife. And even if he were, after his brief, disastrous marriage to Danielle, it would have to be someone pretty special to make him take that chance again.

His thoughts flitted to Rochelle Delany and he scolded himself. He'd spent more time than was rational last night thinking about her and that blasted football game.

It was the last home game of the season, his sophomore year. As usual, he'd warmed the bench for most of the game. The upside to not playing was that it put him in close proximity to the cheerleaders. Namely, Rochelle Delany. The downside to not playing was that she didn't know he existed.

A win that night meant a spot in the playoff games, and the tension that had built throughout the entire fourth quarter exploded when Redford's Crossing scored the winning touchdown with two seconds left on the clock. The crowd was in a frenzy. The school song played loud over the PA system. In the melee that erupted, Rochelle impulsively grabbed him and hugged him hard. Before he'd recovered from the hug, she'd astounded him further by kissing him full on the mouth.

He spent the rest of his high school career dreaming of the day she would kiss him and mean it. It never happened. He didn't have any more of a chance with her now than he had in high school, and he might as well get that through his head.

Their meals arrived and Jace dug in with gusto, chattering around a mouthful of fries. Sandy listened to the rise and fall of his voice, and his heart swelled. How could

Danielle not have wanted this boy?

His cell phone chimed in his pocket. Quickly swallowing his food, he pulled it out and answered. "Hello?"

"Hey, Sandy, it's Austin Delany."

"What can I do for you, Austin?"

"I was just wondering what your thoughts are after looking at the house yesterday?"

Sandy winced. Obviously, Austin hadn't talked to his sister. "I didn't get a chance to look at it."

"You didn't?"

"Your sister informed me that it isn't for sale."

"She *what*?"

"That's what she said. Anyway, I can hold off for a little while if you two need some time to talk it over."

"No, listen, I'll talk to her. I'd really like to get the ball rolling if you're interested. I have some time later this afternoon. I can meet you there today if you're free. Would two o'clock be good?"

"Sure, I can be there at two. I'll see you then."

He slid his phone back into his pocket with mixed emotions. If all went well, he'd be finishing up his current renovation project by the end of next week. It would be nice to have the next big project lined up. But a nagging feeling in his gut told him Rochelle would not be happy to see him today.

"Daddy?" Jace had watched the exchange, his expression crestfallen. "Where do we have to go now?"

He reached across the table and ruffled the beloved, caramel-colored mop. "The plaza."

Rochelle couldn't remember the last time she'd slept until ten o'clock. Of course, she'd spent most of the night wide awake. As it turned out, Gus was an insufferable bed hog. At some point in the night, he'd overtaken the middle of the bed, as immovable as a boulder, and she'd been relegated to a twelve-inch strip on the edge. But it wasn't just that. She simply hadn't been able to shut down her thoughts, to quiet her mind.

She hefted Gus onto the floor and stumbled out to the kitchen. There was much to be done today. But first, she made coffee. Minutes later she poured a cup of fresh brew and sank into a chair at the table, weary to her bones. Russ Swanson hadn't been kidding. She had a lot of work ahead of her, a lifetime of Bessie's paperwork and possessions to sort through.

She ran a loving hand over the battered old table where so many hours of her life had been spent. What she wouldn't give to have one more hour at this table with Bessie. If only she'd listened to Bessie's concerns about her plan to go to California, instead of dismissing them as old fashioned and out of touch. If only she'd taken Bessie's advice and enrolled in classes at the community college instead of buying the computer.

If only, if only . . .

At first, Ro had seen her new computer as a means of escaping, if only for a while, the town that had seemed too small for her. The Internet opened her eyes to things and places she'd never dreamed of. She watched tutorials on hair styling and makeup application. She visited websites and chat rooms, soaked up the glamour and luxury lifestyles of famous stylists in California, becoming more dissatisfied with Redford's Crossing by the day. There was money to be made, and plenty of it, in the beauty industry.

When she came across an ad in a private chat room: *Come to California! Style for the stars! Paid training! Guaranteed work!,* her breath caught and her heart started to pound. For three years, she'd put off her dreams for the family she loved, but with Bessie's cancer finally in remission, Ro felt her time had come at last. This was her ticket out. She just knew it. All that glittered was in California, and all of it could be hers.

She'd thought that fame and fortune would ease the relentless ache inside that told her she wasn't enough. Oh, how she wished she had known then what she knew today.

Over her second cup of coffee, Ro made a to-do list. Her first task would be to pick up some groceries. She'd need more than bagels and most of the food in Bessie's cupboards was well past its expiration date. While she was out, she'd also have to buy a cell phone. And then maybe she'd start sorting Bessie's possessions. The hall closet shouldn't be too daunting. She could start there and see how it went. She set down her pen and carried her cup to the sink. First things first. She'd have to find something to wear. She'd fled California with nothing but the clothes on her back, and she planned to put those in the burn barrel. Hopefully, some of her old clothes still fit.

Flipping through the outfits in her closet, she considered, and then discarded each item she touched. All of it was a decade out of date. No and no. Yoga pants and bright spandex tights. Definitely no. By now, the town grapevine would likely be ripe with gossip about her arrival, and she didn't think she had the strength to make small talk with a bunch of people she no longer knew. Her hope was to get through her errands unnoticed, and none of these outfits would help her do that.

Happily, her old jeans still fit. As a teen, she'd gone through a phase of collecting vintage concert T-shirts. She pulled a faded gray T-shirt from its hanger and considered it. Not exactly her style anymore, but it would have to do.

Bessie's reliable old car was still in the driveway. Austin said they'd have to try and sell it eventually, but she was welcome to use it while she was here. She hadn't driven in almost a decade. She didn't even have a driver's license anymore. When she'd first gone to work for Menzo, he'd taken her ID to make copies of it, and she'd never gotten it back. Only later did she find out that Menzo didn't allow his girls to drive. If she were careful, though, not having a license wouldn't be an issue. She sat behind the wheel for a long moment, getting reacquainted with the car, and then turned the key and backed out into the street.

She'd hoped for a quick pass-through at Wally's Corner Market, where she'd worked so long ago, but when she reached the corner of Orchard Drive and South Main Street she saw with dismay that Wally's had gone out of business. The red and white sign above the door had been removed and what windows weren't broken, were boarded up. With a curious sense of loss, she headed for the supermarket on the other side of town.

The moment she stepped into the grocery store someone called her name. Her plan of going unnoticed was not happening.

Natalie Prescott, her former cheerleading co-captain, hurried toward her.

She forced a smile. "Hello, Nat."

"Is it really you?" she gave Rochelle a hug, then stood back to study her. "I can't believe it. You're even more beautiful now than you were in school."

Natalie had gained a few pounds, but the older version of the girl seemed to have grown into a natural beauty that the younger used to bury under makeup. What was it that Natalie had now that she hadn't, back then?

"So are you," she said truthfully.

"Nah," Natalie waved the compliment away. "I'm just an ordinary mommy. Two boys and a girl. I ended up marrying Bootsie."

Contentment. Natalie possessed the comfortable satisfaction that came with living the life you were meant to live. A status Rochelle doubted she herself would ever achieve.

"Bootsie Brady? No kidding."

"Yep. So I heard you're a model now."

"Ah, not exactly. So, three kids, huh? That must keep you pretty busy."

"It does for sure. Crazy busy. But I love it." Natalie gently touched Ro's arm. "I was so sorry to hear about Bessie. She was always so patient and so kind with us cheerleaders. She was the only one of the mothers that would put up with having all of our girl drama around all the time. I miss her."

"Me, too."

"Will you be in town for a while? I'd love to get together."

"I'm sure we can arrange something."

"Great, let me get your number."

"I lost my cell phone, but I'll get in touch with you soon. Look, I've got to run, but it's great to see you, Nat."

In the produce section, she encountered Lexie Durant.

In the frozen foods aisle, Zoe Cartwright.

Canned Goods. Baking Needs. Cleaning Supplies. Jimmy Garrett. Pattie Whitman. Lainey Morgan. Her head was swimming with their condolences about Bessie, with their questions about Rochelle's life that she did not want to answer. And beneath every word they spoke, she sensed a thinly veiled accusation. She was not here when Bessie needed her. Or maybe she was just imagining it, projecting her own deep feelings of guilt onto these people.

When she turned the car back onto Orchard Drive, it was after two o'clock and she was emotionally drained. Somehow, she'd finished her errands, and now she just wanted to go in the house and hide.

From a block away, she saw the white truck parked in front of Bessie's house. Sandy Fairbrother's truck. What on earth was he doing here?

She pulled in the driveway and carried her groceries inside. From the window, she could see him walking around the backyard, where he appeared to be examining the roof.

Her anger flared. Of all the nerve!

Leaving her grocery bags on the table, she stormed outside to confront him, but stopped short when she noticed the little boy. She drew a breath and counted to ten, holding back the tongue lashing she'd planned to give Sandy. "Can I help you?" she finally asked.

The little boy grinned, two dimples creasing his cheeks. "We're gonna buy Bessie's house!"

Rochelle shot an incredulous look at Sandy.

"Jace," Sandy interjected, "I didn't say —"

"Bessie died," the child said, suddenly looking so sad Ro's heart thawed a little.

"I know she did, honey."

"Daddy says she's in heaven."

"I'm sure she is." Rochelle could barely answer.

"Daddy says someday I'll see her again, and my kitty, Tommy Tiger, too. Can I play with Gus?"

"Not right now, champ," Sandy interjected.

"Actually, I think that's a great idea." Rochelle smiled at the child. "He's right in the kitchen. Why don't you go in and see him? I'm sure he'd love that."

As the boy raced off, she whirled back to Sandy. "How dare you!"

"Look, it isn't —"

"I told you this house is not for sale."

"Yes, you did."

"Then why are you here?"

He blew out a breath. "I talked with your

brother this morning. He said —"

"Austin is only half owner of this house. He doesn't get to decide anything without me. And you don't get to come over here any time you want to, acting as if you already own the place!"

His phone chimed in his pocket. He ignored it. "Look, I'm not trying to cheat anyone here, if that's what you're afraid of. I'll pay a fair price. But I'm sure you can see that this house needs a lot of work."

"It's not about a fair price."

"Then what is it about? You haven't cared about this house — or anyone in it — for years."

The words deflated her. "That's not true."

"Isn't it?" His phone chimed again. "I don't need this house, Rochelle. And you've probably got something ten times more valuable than this in California. But in case you hadn't noticed, your brother has a lot on his plate right now. He asked me to come over, so I'm here. Selling it would help him out in more ways than one. But you're all about yourself. You always have been."

Suddenly she couldn't breathe. She'd heard it, though not so plainly spoken, from half the town this morning. For some reason, coming from this man, it cut through her like a knife. Tears filled her eyes and spilled down her cheeks. "Can you please go now?"

His angry expression melted away and his voice softened. "Look, I'm sorry."

"Forget it."

"I had no right to talk to you that way. I don't know why I did."

"I said forget it."

His phone dinged, alerting him to a voicemail. He took it out, impatiently punched in his code, and put it to his ear. After a moment, he slid it back in his pocket. "You should probably check your phone."

"I don't have one." The lie she'd carefully rehearsed slid smoothly from her lips. "My purse, along with all of my bags, were stolen at the bus station."

"Then you should probably head over to the hospital. Kat's in labor. You're about to become an aunt."

4

She stared at him, uncomprehending. "But Kat isn't due for another two weeks."

"I guess the baby didn't get the memo. I'll grab Jace, and we'll get out of your way."

"Right. I should go." She turned and hurried toward the house, with Sandy following close behind.

Inside, they were met by a horrific odor. Jace looked up from where he sat, petting the dog.

"Gus pooped," he announced.

It was then that Rochelle noticed the dark trail across the kitchen floor, the feces oozing out of Gus' diaper.

"Oh, no!" Rochelle wailed. "Oh, Gus."

"It stinks," Jace said, pinching the end of his nose.

"It's my fault," she said, grabbing a roll of paper towels from the cupboard. "I should have taken him out as soon as I got home."

"I'll clean this up," Sandy said. "You go

ahead and go."

"I can't ask you to do that."

"You didn't. Now go. I've got this."

"Are you sure?"

"Rochelle, I'm sure."

Torn, she thought about it for less than a second. It was preposterous that he would even make such an offer, especially in light of their recent altercation, and if she hadn't been anxious to get to the hospital, she never would have allowed it. But she was going to be an auntie and she didn't want to miss out on a single moment of the adventure.

"OK. Thank you." She hurriedly scooped her hair back into a clip, grabbed her car keys from the table, and rushed out the door.

Twenty minutes later, Rochelle was having second thoughts. She hesitated outside the door of Kat's hospital room, listening for clues as to what was happening inside. She had no idea what the protocol was for this sort of thing. Was it appropriate for her to be here? Was she even wanted?

After several agonized moments, she straightened her shoulders, said a prayer for courage, and poked her head inside. "Knock, knock."

Kat lay in the hospital bed, her long, red

curls slicked with sweat, angry red splotches scattered across her pale, round face. Her eyes lit up when she saw Rochelle.

"Rochelle? Is it you?"

"It's me."

She smiled. "Bring it in, girl."

She opened her arms wide, and Rochelle gratefully moved into them. "You're just as pretty as Bessie said you were, and here I look like a doggone mess."

"You look beautiful." Rochelle was sincere.

"I feel like a wrung-out washrag. But thank you for coming. It means a lot to us."

Seeing the dark expression on her brother's face, Rochelle said, "I know this is an intimate moment and I'll not intrude, I just wanted you to know I'm here. I'll be out in waiting room. Waiting."

"It's not any kind of moment at all, so you just sit right down. The baby's fine and I'm fine. It was false labor pains. It happens sometimes, I guess. They'll keep me another hour or so and then send me home."

Rochelle wasn't sure how to respond. "That's good news, right?"

"I can't say I'm not ready to have this pregnancy over with, but at least this will give Austin time to finish painting the nursery."

49

"This pregnancy has turned you into a real diva, you know." Austin teased. There was no mistaking the love in his expression.

"I can help you with the nursery," Rochelle said quickly. "I love to paint."

"You hear that, babe?" Kat asked. "Looks as if you're off the hook."

"No, I'll do it," Austin said firmly. "I'm sure Rochelle will have her hands full with getting Bessie's house cleaned out before she heads back to California."

For the second time that day, Rochelle's throat clogged with tears. He acted as though he hated her. Why did he have to be so unforgiving?

As Rochelle perched uneasily on a chair, Kat bubbled over with a description of the labor pains she'd experienced.

"I was hanging the sheets out on the line and wham! This pain came from out of nowhere and nearly knocked me off my feet. Twenty minutes later, there was another one, and then another one after that, so I called Austin and here we are. But it's not happening today. Probably not even this week, according to my OB."

Kat was just as delightful as Bessie had said, and Rochelle felt an instant liking for the young woman. Her eyes shining, Kat went on to describe her plans for a baby dinosaur nursery, and the uncomfortable moment passed.

"We like Harley if it's a boy," she finally said. "If it's a girl, we want to name her after Bessie, at least for her middle name."

"You don't know its gender?"

"I don't want to know. I love surprises. Well, except for the surprise of going into labor this morning. The pain was unbelievable, and now I'm flat out terrified to go through with it, to tell you the truth. But God's got this. Even if I don't."

Austin tenderly tucked a strand of hair behind Kat's ear. "I don't think you have any choice, sweetheart. There's no turning back now."

A nurse entered the room. She handed Kat a menu and then took her vital signs.

"Everything good?" Austin asked.

"Everything's fine. The doctor was called in for an emergency C-section, which is why your wife hasn't been discharged yet." She smiled at Kat. "Looks as if it'll be a while. Let's get you something to eat. What looks good?"

Kat perused the menu the nurse had given her. "Since I don't see pepperoni pizza on the menu, I guess I'll go with the fruit cup and a turkey sandwich. Extra mayo, please. And an apple juice."

"Coming right up," the nurse said, exiting the room.

"Austin, you haven't eaten since breakfast," Kat said. "You must be starved."

"I'm fine."

"Why don't you and Rochelle go and grab something from the cafeteria and bring it back here. We can all eat together."

"I'm really not hungry, Kat."

"Babe, I don't want to eat in front of you two. Now go."

"All right, all right." Austin reluctantly stood and walked with Rochelle to the elevator, looking as if he'd rather be anywhere else. As they rode down to the ground floor, Ro tried to engage him in conversation.

"I'm so excited for you two. I can't even imagine . . . You're going to be a father! Can you believe it?"

"Yep."

"I'd be happy to help with the nursery. Or anything else you two need. It's not like I don't have the time."

He stared ahead of him in stony silence.

"You chose well. Kat is so sweet. What a trooper."

The elevator doors slid open and they stepped out.

"Anyway, I picked up a cell phone while I

52

was in town this morning. When the time comes for real, I wish you'd let me —"

"Don't."

"What do you mean?"

"Don't try to act as though you're . . . Just don't."

"As though I'm what? A part of the family?"

"I don't want to talk about this."

"Well I do. I want to know why you're holding onto all of this anger. Why can't you just let it go?"

"All right, we'll talk about my anger." Taking her elbow, he steered her to the side of the hallway, out of the flow of foot traffic. "For starters, why are you trying to stop me from selling the house? Sandy Fairbrother is ready, willing, and able to buy it. Selling it to him would save me the hassle of putting it on the market."

"He sprang it on me out of the blue. You and I hadn't even talked about it."

"What was to talk about? I didn't think you'd care what happened to the house. And frankly the upkeep and property taxes on it are eating me and Kat alive."

"I get that, Austin. I just can't bear the thought of Bessie's home becoming some . . . some rental property."

"Sandy Fairbrother is no slum lord." His

face was turning red, his tone sharp. "He's taken a lot of rundown old dumps in this town and made them into beautiful homes."

"OK. Maybe we should sell it and maybe we shouldn't. The point is I haven't had time to think about all this."

"What's to think about?"

"I was thinking I might want to stay in Redford's Crossing for a while. Get to know your wife, your child."

"You gave up that privilege nine years ago when you walked away from this town and everyone in it. Including your family."

"I know that's the way it seemed."

"How else would it *seem*? You couldn't be bothered to come home for either of my graduations, or even my wedding. You couldn't even return my phone calls. You were obviously done with me so I stopped trying. And you didn't even seem to notice. You wouldn't be here now if not for Bessie's will."

Tears filled her eyes. "That's not true."

"Isn't it?"

"I wanted to come home. I couldn't."

"Until now. I guess what they say is true. Where there's a *will* there's a way."

"There was *no* way, Austin."

"Why not?"

What could she tell him, that she was a

prisoner all those years, living under Menzo Maricello's reign of terror? That while living in Menzo's dark shadow, she lost herself? Yes, she would tell him all of that and more. But not here. And not now.

"And forget about me, because I obviously didn't matter. But how do you think Bessie felt?"

"People leave home, Austin. It's not a crime."

"People leave home, yes. But most people don't just cut all ties to their family. You broke Bessie's heart."

The pain of his words was ferocious. "I'm sorry about that."

"Yeah. So am I. But you can't come strolling in here now and expect us to be one big happy family. I'm sorry, Ro. It's too late for that." Jamming his hands in his pockets, he turned and strode into the cafeteria.

After Rochelle left, Sandy stood in the kitchen, assessing the situation.

"OK, first things first. Let's get you in the bath tub, old man." He removed the soiled diaper and led a reluctant Gus to the bathroom. He filled the tub with lukewarm water, squirted in some flea shampoo he found in the linen cupboard, and lifted the dog in. Gus sat patiently as Sandy gently scrubbed at his hindquarters with a paper towel.

"He likes it!" Jace squealed.

"I don't know that I'd say *likes,* exactly, but at least he's putting up with it."

"Baths are fun, Gussy. Hey, Daddy, can I give Gus a soap beard?"

"I guess so. Just don't get any in his eyes, OK?"

He left Jace happily soaping the dog and went back to the kitchen. Rummaging in the cupboard, he found canister of antiseptic wipes and went to work on the dog mess on the floor. From the open bathroom door, he heard Jace's sing-song voice crooning to the dog.

With the floor cleaned, he stowed the milk and eggs Rochelle had bought in the fridge and placed the other items in the cupboard. He retrieved a pitcher from under the sink and returned to the bathroom. Gus was adequately soaped and looked none too happy about it. Sandy pulled the plug.

"OK, now we have to rinse him off."

"Can I do it?"

"Sure." He turned on the faucet and tested the temperature. "Just be very careful to keep the water the temperature it is. Not too hot, not too cold, just as you like it for your baths, OK?"

"OK."

With the bath finished, Sandy lifted Gus from the tub and toweled him dry. When Gus had thoroughly shaken himself, Sandy set Jace up in a corner of the kitchen with one of Bessie's old hairbrushes.

"He smells good, huh, Dad?"

"Well, he smells better, anyway. Now you have to brush him. Do a good job, all right?"

With Jace happily brushing the dog, Sandy turned his attention to the kitchen sink. Upon inspection, he discovered that the plumbing and all of the fixtures needed to be replaced. His glance swept over the outdated appliances and the chipped countertops. Truth be told, the entire kitchen needed an overhaul, but for now he could at least fix the faucet.

He went out to his truck and retrieved a pair of pliers and a washer from his tool box. Back inside, he turned off the water supply beneath the sink and went to work on the faucet. Unable to resist tools of any kind, Jace wandered over. "Can I help you, Dad?"

"Sure, you can hold my tools for me."

He clamped on the pliers and gently turned them until the aerator came loose from the spout, then removed the old washer and inspected it.

"I like playing with Gus," Jace said. "I wish we could have him."

"He doesn't belong to us, Champ. This is his home, but maybe you can come and play with him sometimes."

"Who was that lady?"

He wiped what looked like a year's worth of gunky residue from the fitting. "That's Bessie's daughter."

"She's pretty."

He set in the new washer and threaded the aerator back into place. "Yes, she is. Hand me my pliers, OK?"

"She was mad at us."

"Not at you, Champ. At me."

"How come?"

"Grownups get mad sometimes, just like kids do. It's nothing for you to worry about, all right?"

"OK. I miss Bessie."

"I know you do."

"Are we gonna buy her house? We could live here with Gus and Bessie's daughter."

Sandy laughed and ruffled his son's hair. "I don't think that's gonna happen, Jace."

"Why not?"

"It just isn't." He gently screwed the spout back in place, turned on the water beneath the sink, and then turned on the faucet. He slowly increased the water pressure. The spout held. "OK, it's time to say goodbye to Gus. We're all done here."

Back home, he settled Jace in front of his favorite cartoon, poured a glass of iced tea, and carried it to the porch. He'd acted like all kinds of a fool today. He'd made Rochelle cry, and the memory of her tears sliced through him like a blade. What had gotten into him, to say those things to her? It was bad enough he'd thought them at all, but to say them out loud? There was no excuse for that, no matter how angry she'd made him.

He took a swallow of tea. There was no way to take the words back, but maybe he could find a way to lessen their impact. In any case, if she felt that strongly about not selling the house, he'd back off. He'd tell Austin he wasn't interested in it after all.

He sighed. He'd have another sleepless night, with those tears on his conscience. It was still early. Maybe he'd call Danielle's mother, Sue, and ask if she'd sit with Jace for a little while this evening. Then he'd stop by Bessie's house and tell Rochelle again that he was sorry. And he'd pray to God she'd forgive him.

That evening, Rochelle was still reeling from her confrontation with Austin. Would she ever be able to win back his trust?

Memories rose up and tormented her. Haunting images of Austin and her playing in the yard on long-ago summer days, or working on jigsaw puzzles together on cold winter nights, snug and safe under Bessie's roof. And before Bess took them in, those terrifying days after their parents went to the store and never returned, when Rochelle had done her best to take care of him. Their mutual dependence on each other had created a bond most siblings never achieved. It was her and Austin against the world. But now they were against each other, and the disintegration of that bond was like a thousand shards of glass shattering in her heart.

Weary, she rested her head against the back of the couch, the ticking of the grandfather clock the only sound. For the first time she could remember, the house felt lonely and haunted.

"God," she whispered. "I know I've been out of touch. I know I've made a mess of things and I'm sorry. Please, if You're listening, could You please help me straighten out my life?"

A sudden, sharp knock at the door sent her heart to her throat.

Calm down. It's probably just the Swansons again.

Without turning on the light, she moved to the window and peeked out. Sandy Fairbrother stood on the porch. She opened the door. From his startled look, she must have looked a mess, her face wrecked from her afternoon crying binge. "Hi, Sandy."

"What happened? Is the baby OK?"

"The baby's fine. It was a false alarm. They sent Kat back home."

"Oh, good. That's good, right?"

"Yes."

He shifted his weight, stuffed his hands in his pockets, and then drew them out again. "Listen, Rochelle, about the things I said earlier. I want to apologize."

She waved a dismissive hand. "It's all right."

"No, it's not." A moth fluttered in front of his face and he swatted it away. "Could I come in for a minute?"

She stood aside and he moved past her into the hallway.

"Thank you for cleaning up after Gus today," she said. "And for fixing my sink."

"It was nothing."

"Would you like a cold drink? A cola or an iced tea?"

"Sure, if you're having one."

In the kitchen, she filled two glasses with ice, opened a bottle of cola, and poured them each a glass. "Your little boy is adorable."

The comment seemed to put him at ease. "He's a great kid. I'd say that even if he weren't my son."

She took a seat at the table and motioned him to sit. "How does he know Gus?"

"When Jace started school, his teacher noticed he wasn't catching on to reading as he should be. I asked around and the consensus was that Bess would be the best one to tutor him, so I reached out to her. Jace and I spent every Tuesday evening here for months. After the tutoring sessions, Bess and I would talk and Jace would play with Gus. Sometimes Bess and Jace would play Crazy Eights. We'd always have dinner together." He smiled. "Bess made enough food to feed the whole town. I guess she thought we needed fattening up."

"Your wife doesn't cook?"

"I'm divorced."

"Ahh," she said, and was immediately ashamed of the strange thrill the confession gave her.

"How about you?"

"I never married."

He nodded.

She tipped her glass to her lips, swallowed, and set it back on the table. "Did Bess ever talk about me on those Tuesday nights?"

"All the time."

"Really?"

"She was so proud of you. She told us all about the fancy salon you worked in, said you even did make-up for movie stars."

Her gaze went to her hands. "It wasn't a big deal. B grade movies."

"Still, pretty impressive for a little ol' Redford's Crossing girl." He took a swallow from his glass and set it back down. "She worried about you, though. She had the sense that something wasn't right. We said a lot of prayers for you at this table." He rapped the tabletop with his knuckles.

She didn't answer, didn't trust herself to speak. Tears threatened again. She'd written to Bessie as often as she'd dared to, furtive letters scribbled in the post office lobby. She'd tried to make her life seem wonderful and exciting, not wanting Bessie to worry. But Bessie, wise, wonderful Bessie, had seen through the charade.

You broke her heart . . .

She couldn't bear to know, but could no longer bear not to. "Was she angry with me, Sandy?"

His eyebrows shot up. "Bessie? Good

Lord, no. She loved you, Rochelle, even if she didn't always understand your choices."

"Thank you for telling me. That makes me feel better."

"Is that what's bothering you? None of my business but it looks as though you've been crying."

She let out a shaky breath. "Unlike Bessie, my brother is very angry with me. I think he's disowned me, to tell you the truth."

"He'll come around."

"I hope you're right. I don't really blame him if he doesn't. But it's still very painful."

"I get it."

"Do you?"

"I don't have much of a relationship with my own family. None at all, actually. My parents moved to Florida a few years back. We don't talk. I wish it could be different, for Jace's sake. He's got his Grandma Sue, my ex-wife's mother, and she's good to him. But I'd like him to have two sets of grandparents. Aunts, uncles, cousins, the whole bit."

"You said you have a brother. Aren't you close with him?"

"That's a long story."

"I've got time," she said softly.

He hesitated for a long moment. "My father was tough. He worked hard and he drank even harder. And when he drank, it was a nightmare for me and my brother. My mother never stood up to him. I suppose she was afraid to. My older brother, Joe, got the worst of it. Nothing he ever did was good enough. He joined the army at eighteen to escape. I was too young for the army, so I joined the football team. It gave me a way to be out of the house. And at least on the field I knew when the punishment was coming."

She thought of the young boy who seemed content to sit on the sidelines. She'd thought it was out of a love for the game.

"I never saw my brother again after that. I don't know where Joe is, or even *if* he's alive. But not a day goes by that I don't miss him."

"I'm sorry."

"I hope you and Austin can get past whatever's between you."

"Me, too."

"Is it about the house? Because you don't have to decide anything right away. I have a couple of other prospects."

"It's not entirely about the house. But thank you."

"None of my business, but why do you want to hang onto this place so badly?"

He'd been forthright with her. And very

kind. She should return the favor, but she couldn't bring herself to tell him the truth, not all of it.

"I just want to feel as if I have a place to come home to. Maybe that sounds childish."

"It's not childish at all."

"Anyway, it's not even officially ours yet. Although we both were aware of the will's contents, the reading of the will is scheduled for this Tuesday. Usually, there isn't a reading of the will, because the executor is supposed to carry out the wishes of the person, but Bessie wanted her lawyer to administer everything."

"I know. I got a letter."

"You did?"

"I'm thinking Bess probably left some little thing to Jace. She always said knowing he needed her gave her the strength to keep fighting the cancer. They had a very special bond."

"It would be just like her to leave him something." A thought occurred to Ro and she giggled.

"What?"

"You don't suppose she left him Gus, do you?"

"I hope not."

His expression was so horrified she burst

66

out laughing.

"Thanks," he said wryly.

"I'm sorry."

"Yeah, I can tell."

That made her laugh even harder. She couldn't remember the last time she'd laughed. "What will you do?"

"If she wanted us to have him, we'd have to take him. I guess we'll cross that bridge if we come to it."

She laughed again, and this time he laughed with her. Finally, almost reluctantly, he stood. "I'd better get back and rescue Jace's grandma." Retrieving a napkin and a pen from the table, he jotted down a number. "This is my cell number. When you get a new phone, put this in it. And if you need any help around here while you're home, please feel free to call me."

She smiled. "I appreciate that."

Then he was gone and the house was quiet again, but it no longer felt haunted and neither did she. There was something calming about his presence. Something soothing. Bessie had trusted Sandy Fairbrother with her secrets. Maybe Ro could, too.

5

Despite Gus hogging the bed, Rochelle awoke on Sunday morning feeling refreshed and ready for the day ahead. The uneasy feeling that had shadowed her since she arrived, the feeling that Bessie had died angry with her, was gone, and she had Sandy to thank for that. The added bonus was that her kitchen sink was no longer a shower. She would find a way to repay him.

After breakfast, and a long, slow soak in the tub, she put up her hair, threw on a pair of jeans, and a concert T-shirt. Armed with plenty of trash bags and a few produce boxes she'd gotten from the grocery store the day before, she went to tackle the hall closet.

Opening the double doors, she considered the plethora of items inside. Bessie might have delegated some of the personal items in her will, so Ro had to be careful what she discarded. But she could certainly donate coats and boots to the homeless shelter.

Stuffing most into bags, Ro saved a pair of boots and two coats she'd worn in the past for herself, she moved on to the basket of hats, gloves, and scarves. The broken vacuum cleaner and the VCR could go out with the trash, and she'd donate the extra blankets to the animal shelter. After an hour, the closet was empty except for a few shoe boxes on the top shelf. Dragging a chair in from the kitchen, she took the boxes down.

The first one held decades-old Christmas and birthday cards from friends and relatives. Hopelessly sentimental, it didn't look as if Bessie had ever thrown a single greeting card away.

Setting the cards aside, Ro opened the second box and discovered more of the same. As she opened the third box, her breath carved a painful path through her chest. This one contained Rochelle's letters.

Pulling in a breath, she removed the thin stack and flipped through them. Several were wrinkled and torn, and not simply because they had been read and reread a dozen times. The all too familiar words scrawled in the corners of those letters nearly made her ill. *Damaged in transit.*

In her first weeks in California, many of

the letters she had received from Bessie had born those same words. It had taken a while for her to catch on that the letters had not been torn open by a careless postal worker. Menzo had opened them and read each and every word.

I had my interview today, Bessie. I've been accepted into the training program! Only a few out of dozens of girls made the cut, and I was one of them! I'll start my training in a few days, and after I earn my certificate there'll be no stopping me!

What a little fool she'd been! On that first day, sitting across from Menzo in the lobby of his hotel, she'd thought her answers to his questions made her seem savvy and independent; that she had no parents, no family, and that she could take care of herself. There was no way to deny that she came from a small town in Ohio. Menzo had her application sitting right in front of him. She'd feared that coming from a small Appalachian town in the middle of nowhere would make her seem unsophisticated. Little did she know that all of those things added up to make her exactly the kind of vulnerable, naïve girl Menzo was looking for.

The memory gutted her. Without reading the rest, she tore the letters to shreds and dropped them in the kitchen trash can. Gus looked up from his pillow with a questioning glance.

"From now on, no reminders, Gus," she told him.

He wagged his rear end in response.

"As much as I wish I could, I can't change the past. But I can go forward. I'm making a new life. Starting today."

With the hall closet finished, she moved on to the bathroom, filling bags with half empty jars of face creams and dried out bottles of nail polish. The clean, empty space energized her, somehow, and she decided to keep going.

The attic crawl space was stacked to the ceiling with boxes, all of them containing Christmas decorations; decades of Bessie's lovely handcrafts, Ro and Austin's handmade ornaments, and who knew what else. She gazed at the carefully labeled containers, all at once feeling overwhelmed. Christmas had been Bessie's favorite holiday, and she'd decorated every last inch of the house. Sorting through these boxes of memories would take more stamina than she possessed today. Still, she grabbed the one marked *Bessie's Stained-Glass Creations* and carried it down the ladder and to the living room. Pulling back the flaps, she removed the first treasure; a stained-glass angel in palest pink. The second was a milky white snowman, his hat and scarf a cobalt blue. There were delicate snowflakes and jolly Santas, golden stars, and little white churches, all of the details stunning and precise. Bessie could have easily sold her ornaments for a good profit at the holiday craft fairs, but chose instead to give them away to friends. She insisted that her work was purely for joy, not for profit. Selecting a gold nutcracker with a bright red jacket, Ro set it aside for Jan Swanson.

As she repacked the box, an idea came to her and she smiled. Redford's Crossing's love affair with Christmas was one of the things she'd missed the most while in California. The day after Thanksgiving, every porch, storefront window, and streetlamp in town came alive with glittering lights and cheerful banners. Most dazzling of all was Main Street Park. For as long as Ro could remember, the local tree farmers had donated dozens of scotch pines and blue spruce to the city at Christmas time, delivering them to the park for townspeople to decorated in honor of loved ones who had passed away. This year, she would do a stained-glass memory tree in Bessie's honor. She would enlist Kat and Austin's help and make the tree a showcase for Bessie's wonderful creations! What better way to honor Bessie's memory? She tucked the box back in the attic, warmed by thoughts of holiday parades and steaming mugs of cocoa, of caroling under the streetlamps and candlelit manger scenes. Of her first Christmas back home.

Later that afternoon, she hauled a dozen bulging trash bags to the car, drove across town, and dropped them in the donation boxes at the homeless shelter and the dog pound. She drove home feeling satisfied with her day's work.

In the kitchen, she brewed a cup of coffee and sat down at the table. There was just one thing left on her to-do list. Retrieving the napkin Sandy had written his cell number on, she added it to her contacts in her new phone. It wasn't that she was interested in him, she told herself as she pressed the call button. It was just that he'd been so kind. She owed him. And besides, this new life of hers would be lonely without a friend or two.

The call went to voicemail, and she hung up without leaving a message. Within moments, her phone rang.

"Hello?"

"Rochelle?"

"Yes."

"So it is you."

"What?"

"I saw a missed call, thought it might be you. Is everything OK?"

"Everything's fine. I called because I worked up an appetite cleaning out Bessie's closets today, and I wondered if you'd like to come for dinner tonight, you and Jace. It seems like a good night for spaghetti and meatballs."

He hesitated for long enough that she felt foolish. She shouldn't have called him, but there was no taking it back now.

"I'm no Bess Casey in the kitchen, but I can hold my own. And I thought Jace might like to play with his new dog."

He laughed softly. "I'd really like that, and I'm sure Jace would too. The thing is we generally go to church on Sunday evenings. We're not great about getting up early on Sunday mornings, so the later service works better for us."

"Oh. We'll do it another time, then."

"Yeah, that sounds great. Unless . . . I mean . . . would you want to go with us?"

"To church?"

He laughed. "Yeah."

"I guess I could, but I don't have anything to wear." It was horribly cliché, but in her case, it was the truth.

"I don't think the good Lord will care what you're wearing, Rochelle. And Jace and I certainly won't."

"Right. Sure, then, I'd love to go. Why not?"

"Great. We'll stop by for you around a quarter to six."

She clicked off the call and checked the time. It was 4:15. After a quick shower, she went through the shirts in her closet again, deciding on a pale pink tee. Pulling it over her head, she wrinkled her nose. It smelled a bit like moth balls. She'd come across a bottle of body splash in Bessie's bathroom. Not exactly her first choice of fragrance, but it was better than nothing, so she hurriedly sprayed some on.

At 5:45 on the nose, when Sandy knocked on her door, she was relieved to see that he also wore jeans and a T-shirt.

"I see you found something to wear," he joked.

"I'll definitely have to do some shopping soon."

"The morning service is pretty traditional, but the evening services are casual. That's another reason I prefer them for Jace. It's usually geared toward the church's youth, with lots of instruments and hand clapping.

Jace loves the music."

"I'm sure it will be great."

He drove across town to a small, red-brick church she'd passed hundreds of times but never been inside. The sign above the door said simply, Redford's Crossing Christian Church. The evening's congregation was made up of mostly children, 'tweens, teens, and their parents. She followed Sandy to a pew near the front. When they were seated, Jace wriggled into the space between them.

The service began with a few lively choruses, complete with the promised hand clapping and tambourines, and then the youth pastor, a nice-looking man in his early twenties, said an opening prayer. "I see a couple of new faces out there tonight. Welcome. It's good to have you here."

His gaze rested for a moment on Rochelle, and she cringed inside. Growing up in Bessie's church, visitors were always asked to stand and introduce themselves. She was relieved when the pastor's gaze returned to the teenagers in the front row.

"So! I've got a question for you tonight. Who here thinks they have the guts to be a Daniel?" he asked.

No one answered, but every face was turned toward him in anticipation.

"Who is Daniel, you ask? Daniel was an

ordinary guy, just like you. He made a lot of choices every day, a thousand of which he didn't even think about; what to eat for dinner, what music to listen to, what to wear. Like you, most of Daniel's choices didn't seem like a big deal. But imagine all of them being taken away. Imagine that tomorrow the ruler of another country comes and takes you away from your family and everything that's familiar and comfortable. Sounds rough, huh? Welcome to Daniel's world."

Rochelle had expected the familiar disconnect she'd often experienced while sitting in church with Bessie as a young girl. Instead, she found herself strangely riveted to the young pastor's words.

"Daniel wasn't much older than some of you when he and his pals were carted off to a place called Babylon by a king named Nebuchadnezzar. They spoke a freaky language in Babylon. They wore weird clothes. They even changed Daniel's name to *Belteshazzar*."

Laughter rippled across the church.

"Belteeshazzer," Jace echoed, snuggling against her side. Ro dropped her arm around his small shoulders.

"You see the rulers wanted to brainwash Daniel and his friends. They wanted to make them fit into his mold. They promised them power and money and popularity. If these captives obeyed the laws of the land. But if they didn't . . ." He drew an imaginary line across his throat.

The words resonated deep within Ro and she shifted uncomfortably. Suddenly the room seemed very warm.

"And Daniel went along with it, to a point. He wore the weird clothes. He learned to speak the freaky language. He even answered to his new name. As far as he was concerned, they could call him whatever they liked. He knew who he really was. But then they tried to give him fancy foods that God had told his people not to eat, and Daniel drew the line and ate vegetables instead. They told him he couldn't pray to his God, our God. They told him he had to pray to Darius, but Daniel didn't care that he might get caught, or that he might get punished. Daniel prayed to God. He didn't pray to Darius. What?" He affected a look of horror. "Oh, no, he didn't!"

"Oh, no, he didn't'!" Jace chimed in joyfully.

"You see, Daniel didn't worry about being *unpopular*. He didn't worry that people would call him a *hater*. He didn't make up excuses for why it would be OK to do something he knew in his heart was wrong. The Bible says Daniel purposed in his heart to obey God. Even if that meant being ridiculed. Even if it meant he wouldn't get the power and the money and the prestige. Even if it meant being killed.

"Was Daniel ever afraid? You bet he was! But he'd made up his mind. He was God's man. It took guts to tell the world's most powerful king, 'Hey, I'm not eating your food. I'm not drinking your wine. No matter what you do to me, I'm doing my life God's way!' "

The message was devastating. Rochelle almost couldn't breathe. Memories of the awful things she'd been a part of flooded over her. The hollow eyes of the girls she'd made up for Menzo's pictures and movies. The pictures she'd posed for, herself. She'd been sickened, filled with self-hatred, but too terrified to refuse. If she'd heard this message ten years ago, would it have made a difference?

"And God rewarded Daniel. He gave Daniel the ability to interpret dreams. He made him the strongest, healthiest boy in the kingdom. When they threw Daniel in the lion's den, God shut the lion's mouths!

"Let me tell you something, folks, God

honors those who honor him. So it's time to make up your mind. This world wants to brainwash you. Make up your mind to say no! No to cigarettes, and yes to healthy bodies. No to dirty movies and websites, and yes to clean minds. No to laying down for the crowd, and yes to standing up for God! No to drug parties, and yes to church. No to promiscuity, and yes to waiting for marriage! No to the *prison* of your sins, and yes to the *freedom found in Jesus Christ!*"

While the church around her erupted in applause and hallelujahs, Rochelle fought tears. How she wished she could go back. Undo the choices she'd made that took her down the dark path she'd walked for nearly a decade. Take back the hurt she'd caused her family. *Forgive me. Oh, please, forgive me.*

The pastor's voice was softer now. "Not many of us are as faithful as Daniel was. We fall. We make mistakes. The good news is, we get a do-over, and that's because God sent His Son to make us new. Are you ready to do it God's way, church? Maybe you made that choice a while ago, but your heart's grown cold. Maybe you never made that choice at all. But if you want to start fresh today, I invite you . . . He invites you . . . come."

Somewhere a guitar strummed softly. Rochelle began to sob. All of the feelings she'd struggled to keep in, every emotion she'd fought to hide from Menzo, and from herself, because her survival depended on it, found release. Here, in the safety of a little brick church, it all came pouring out. With a pull on her heart too strong to resist, Rochelle walked up to the altar to pray. As she knelt, she had no words, only a river of tears streaming from her eyes, and a deep, wrenching, heart-longing to be clean. And then, suddenly, she had Sandy. His warm, strong hand rested ever so gently on her shoulder as he knelt with her, supporting her with his prayers.

And God working on her heart.

How was this evening happening?

Three days ago, the best Sandy had hoped for was a glimpse of this amazing woman who'd lived only in his memories. Now she sat beside him, smelling like suntan lotion, the glow of her encounter with God still lighting up her face.

As they pulled away from the church parking lot, Jace broke the spell.

"Daddy, can we get a milkshake at Maddy's?"

"Good heavens," Rochelle said, "Is

Maddy's still in business? We cheerleaders used to hang out there after all of the football games."

"Yep, it's still open. And it probably hasn't changed a whole lot since the last time you were there."

"Does Maddy Sheridan still own it?"

"She does."

"Daddy can we get a milkshake? Pleeease?"

"She was the best cook in the world, but she could be so crabby sometimes." Rochelle laughed. "I was always kind of afraid of her. Were you there that night, I think it was after the playoff game senior year when Bobby Mitchell took the ketchup packets and —"

"Milkshake!" Jace screamed from the back seat. "Milkshake! Milkshake! Milkshake!"

"Hey!" Sandy thundered, "Enough!"

There was silence from the back seat, followed by the sound of sniffling. It wasn't often that Sandy was stern with the boy. It wasn't often that he needed to be, and he always felt badly after the fact.

After a few long moments, Rochelle murmured, "I sure do love Maddy's milkshakes."

"I sure do love Maddy's milkshakes, too," came a small voice from behind them. "I wish I could have one."

"Sandy hid a smile. "I'll think about it. Do you think that you can be a good boy and apologize to Rochelle for interrupting?"

"I'm sorry."

"It's OK, sweetheart."

"I wanna be a good boy. Just like Daniel."

Rochelle looked at Sandy then, a *cuteness overload* expression on her face. "I'm sure you do."

They walked into Maddy's a half hour before closing time. Thankfully, because of the late hour, Maddy Sheridan was not there. Sandy didn't want the evening to be spoiled by the disapproval he knew he would see written on the older woman's face. Not that half the town wouldn't be buzzing tomorrow about seeing him and Rochelle there together. Ironic that he'd tried to pray this very scenario into existence as a teenager. He smiled. God had taken fifteen years to answer his prayer. But Sandy wasn't complaining.

When their milkshakes arrived, Jace greedily slurped on his straw. "I'm gonna be a Daniel!" he announced.

"You are, huh?"

"Yep. But why did God not want Daniel to eat the fancy foods? Can I still drink milkshakes?"

"I think that would probably be all right," Sandy told him.

"And eat fish sticks, and chicken nuggets?"

"How about macaroni and cheese?" Rochelle asked. "I'm thinking of having you over for dinner sometime soon. I make a pretty good one."

"I like mac and cheese," Jace said, bouncing in his seat. "And chocolate pie."

"Don't push it kid," Sandy told him.

Jace stared at him in consternation, and Rochelle laughed out loud. If he wasn't mistaken, Sandy thought he could see the sparkle returning to her eyes. He was nearly suffocating in her beauty, her big, brown eyes and her glossy black hair tumbling over her shoulders and halfway down her back. Even in an old T-shirt, she was devastatingly beautiful.

By the time Sandy pulled into Bessie's driveway, Jace was practically bouncing out of his booster seat. "Can I play with Gus?"

"Absolutely not. Tonight's a school night, mister. You wait for me right here."

As he walked her to the porch, Rochelle smiled softly. "I think you might be in for a long night."

"I'm kind of getting that same feeling."

"Thank you for tonight," she said. "I loved

84

the service."

"Thank you for going with us."

"We'll have to arrange an evening for that macaroni and cheese dinner soon. And I think I saw that deck of Crazy Eights in the junk drawer."

"Sounds good."

"OK. Well, then, I guess I'll see you on Tuesday."

"Tuesday?"

"The reading of the will?"

"Oh, right. Tuesday." Sandy hesitated, feeling awkward. "Well, good night."

"Good night." She closed the door behind her.

Sandy stepped off the porch, feeling lighter than air. Tuesday. He could hardly wait.

That night, Rochelle took Bessie's old Bible down from the bookcase. Flipping through its pages, she came across passages on guilt and forgiveness, on freedom and oppression. The words she'd heard earlier about the prison of sins and the freedom found in Christ came back to her. She certainly felt as though she'd been let out of prison . . .

From almost day one, Menzo had started to enslave her. Over the years, he gained more and more control over her life, ruling her with an iron fist of fear until she had no fight left in her. She and so many others. She soon learned that the salon was just the tip of the iceberg of Menzo Maricello's empire of massage parlors, black market movies, and seedy hotels. He was a powerful man and a harsh taskmaster. Each of his girls was merely small cogs in a very big wheel that Menzo kept a firm grip on.

Rochelle was never given the lavish paychecks she'd been promised, but Menzo offered her cash, cash she desperately needed, to pose for photos for his ads. She didn't think about the photos, told herself she was not that girl, skimpily dressed, her radiant smile half hidden by a fan of one-hundred dollar bills. *Be a Makeup Artist for the Stars! Free housing! Paid Training! Guaranteed Work!*

Tears ran down her face as she thought about how many other naïve young girls she had probably led away from their families and down Menzo's dark path. How many lives had she helped Menzo destroy?

She knew in her heart God had forgiven her. She'd felt it earlier that night, standing at the altar. She only hoped that with time she could forgive herself.

Two days later when she walked into the

law office of Robert A. McCormick, it was her brother's forgiveness she was thinking of. She hadn't seen Austin since he walked away from her in the hospital on Saturday afternoon. She hoped he would be civil. She was only now starting to feel better about her life and the last thing she wanted was another ugly altercation with her brother.

She approached the pleasant, middle-aged woman who sat at the reception desk. "I'm here for the reading of my foster mother's will."

The woman smiled. "You must be Rochelle. Go on back to Bob's office, hon. Everyone else is already here."

"Thank you."

Tucking a stray strand of hair behind her ear, she headed down the hallway. A deacon at Bessie's church and a longtime friend, Bob McCormick had seen to Bessie's investments for years. Bess had trusted him with the dispensation of her assets, and he would follow her instructions to the letter. Bessie hadn't had much in the way of material possessions, so Rochelle expected the meeting to be brief. Maybe afterwards she and Austin could go out for a cup of coffee or a late lunch, and she would present her plan for buying his share of the house.

The office was small and undecorated

except for a potted fern and a scattering of watercolor prints on the walls. It was only April, but Bob's frugal rejection of air conditioning made the room feel close and hot.

Kat smiled when Ro walked in, looking lovely in black leggings and a coral-colored maternity top. Austin wore his suit and tie, which told her he'd come straight from work. Her gaze went to Sandy and her breath hitched. His hair looked freshly cut, and he'd traded his work clothes for a white button-down shirt and a pair of gray dress pants. She hadn't known it would be a formal occasion and felt sloppy in her T-shirt and yesterday's jeans.

Bob McCormick sat behind his desk, a tidy stack of envelopes in front of him. "Welcome, Rochelle. Now that we're all here, we can get started. Firstly, I'd like to express my condolences. As you know, Bess was not just my client, she was a dear friend, and she will be greatly missed."

Their collective murmurs rippled through the room.

"Bess made some changes to her will shortly before she passed on. There's a letter here for each of you, which I will give to you after the will's been read. If you have any questions, feel free to stop me, but as wills go, this one is pretty straightforward."

He cleared his throat and put on a pair of black-rimmed reading glasses. Rochelle glanced at the envelopes on his desk, one of them containing Bess' last words to her. A bead of sweat trickled down her back.

"Ohio Last Will and Testament of Bess Frances Brown Casey. Pursuant to Chapter 2107 (Wills)," he began.

"I, Bess Frances Brown Casey, resident in the city of Redford's Crossing, County of Jasper, State of Ohio, being of sound mind, not acting under duress or undue influence, and fully understanding the nature and extent of all my property, and of this disposition thereof, do hereby make, publish and declare this document to be my Last Will and Testament, and hereby revoke any and all other wills and codicils heretofore made by me." His glance rested on each of them in turn.

Austin gave a small nod and Bob continued.

"Article one. Expenses and taxes. I direct that all my debts, and expenses of my last illness, funeral, and burial, be paid as soon after my death as may be reasonable convenient, and I hereby authorize my Personal Representative, herein after appointed, to settle and discharge, in his or her absolute discretion, any claims made against my estate . . ."

Rochelle's thoughts drifted from the boring legalese back to the envelopes. She knew without a doubt that anything she might inherit here today was of little value compared to what her envelope contained — Bessie's last, precious thoughts toward her.

"I further direct . . ."

Sandy had assured her that Bess was not angry with her. Even so, a knot of uneasiness tightened in her stomach. What if Bess had thoughts she didn't share with Sandy? How had she really felt? Ro would soon find out.

"Article two, personal representative. I nominate and appoint Robert A. McCormick, of Redford's Crossing, county of Jasper, state of Ohio as Personal Representative of my estate, my trusted friend, and brother in Christ."

His voice cracked. Clearing his throat, he continued.

"Article Three, Disposition of property. I devise and bequeath my property, both real and personal and wherever situated as follows:

To the Literacy Society of Jasper County, I bequeath the sum of two thousand dollars.

To the Redford's Crossing United Fellowship Church, I bequeath the sum of three thousand dollars.

My personal and household possessions, including assets from my investment and retirement accounts, in the sum of thirty-six thousand dollars, are to be divided equally between my beloved children, Austin James Delany and Rochelle Grace Delany, with the exception of:

To Katrina May Delany, I bequeath my collection of Hummel figurines."

Kat cried out softly, tears spilling down her face. Austin dropped his arm around her shoulders and gave them a squeeze.

"To Rochelle Grace Delany, I bequeath one silver quarter-carat diamond engagement ring.

To Austin James Delany I bequeath one vintage Harley Davidson motorcycle, which belonged to my beloved husband, Carl.

To Jace Joseph Fairbrother, minor child of Sandor Ross Fairbrother, I bequeath my beloved pet bulldog, Gustoff."

She heard Sandy's soft sigh and did not dare look at him. She would laugh with him later, she thought, and offer of course, to keep Gus at the house and let Jace come and play with him whenever he wanted.

And then Robert A. McCormick dropped

a second bomb.

"And finally, the real estate property located at 288 Orchard Drive, City of Redford's Crossing, County of Jasper, State of Ohio, I bequeath to Sandor Ross Fairbrother."

6

Rochelle sat woodenly in her chair, trying to make sense of what she'd just heard. It had to be some sort of mistake. Bessie had left the house to Sandy Fairbrother? An outsider?

In a haze of confusion, she saw Austin shake Bob McCormick's hand, and then Sandy's. Then she felt Kat's warm hand on her arm.

"Are you OK, Ro?" Kat asked.

She managed what she hoped was a convincing smile. "I'm fine."

"Wow. That was quite a surprise, huh?"

"Yes, it certainly was."

"Austin and I are pretty relieved to be out from under the worry and the expense of the house. You know, with the baby coming and all. It was a lot to deal with."

"I'm sure you are."

"Anyway, I'm hoping you and I can have lunch together soon, before the baby's born.

I'd love to have a chance to get to know you better."

"I'd like that too, Kat."

"I can't believe Bessie left me her Hummels. I'm ridiculously excited. I've always loved them. Of course I'll have to keep them put up for quite a few years." She patted her tummy. "But still."

"I'll get them wrapped and boxed up for you this week."

"Oh, there's no hurry. I'm gonna be super busy with getting the nursery ready and all . . ."

The rest of her words faded out. Rochelle couldn't take them in, couldn't process another thing. Not when her world was falling apart. The heat in the room was suddenly oppressive. Fearing she'd be ill, she turned and hurried out the door.

She walked past the reception desk and into the blessedly cool spring air. She made it across the parking lot and was almost to Bessie's car when she heard Sandy call her name. Opening her bag, she dug frantically for her car keys.

"Rochelle, wait up!" He sprinted over to her and held out an envelope, a questioning look in his eyes. "You forgot your letter."

"You knew."

"No. I didn't."

"That's why you were so nice about it, so accommodating, isn't it? That's probably why you fixed the sink."

He looked as if she'd slapped him. "What?"

"You knew you already owned the house. You knew we'd find out soon enough so you didn't say a word. That way you didn't have to be the bad guy."

"There's no bad guy here. There's just a crazy set of circumstances that I didn't —"

"What did you and Bessie really talk about, all those Tuesday nights?"

"I already told you what we talked about."

She was like a cornered animal, lashing out. She didn't know if she was being unreasonable or not, but she could not seem to stop the flow of hateful words that spewed from her mouth. She'd trusted this man, and that was what hurt most of all. "You turned her against us. Me and Austin both."

His expression turned to one of disbelief. "Are you kidding me right now?"

"Do I look like I'm kidding?"

"You can't really think that."

"What else *can* I think?" She felt hysteria rising in her throat and struggled to keep her composure.

"Just so you know Austin's perfectly fine

95

with this."

"Of course he's fine with it! To him the house was nothing but a burden. But to me it was everything. It was my *home,* Sandy." Tears stung her eyes and she furiously blinked them back.

"You can stay in the house for as long as you want to. We'll work something out."

"Well, thank you very much!"

"Look, I've only had about ten minutes to get used to this idea. I'd like to read Bess' letter and see what her intentions were before I decide anything."

"I'll be out tomorrow. Is that soon enough?"

"Rochelle."

"Goodbye, Sandy." She grabbed the letter from his hand, got in the car, and sped from the parking lot.

When she arrived home, she was trembling. She set Bessie's letter on the fireplace mantel. She couldn't open it yet. She was too afraid of what it might contain. The astounding news had fractured her newfound positivity. One more upset would break her completely.

She sank down onto the couch. Gus padded into the room, regarded her for a long moment, and then settled at her feet and rested his head on her knee. She absently stroked his ears. "Your new master's a real piece of work, you know that? I honestly thought he cared about me."

Gus sighed.

"What's going to become of me, Gus?"

For the second time in her life, she was backed into a corner. No way out and no way home . . .

She'd known from her first weeks in California that something was very wrong with the arrangement. After her interview, she'd eagerly signed documents agreeing to work for Menzo in exchange for her training. She'd thought she hit the lottery; paid training, free room and board, and guaranteed work, just as the advertisement had promised. But when she and eight other girls were driven from Menzo's hotel to their "dorm," she had her first inkling that her lavish dreams had become a nightmare. She walked through the old, ugly house she would share with these strangers; the outdated kitchen, the mildewed bathroom, and most disappointing, her "private bedroom," a dark little cube with one small window that overlooked a parking lot. The house did not match her beautiful daydreams about how life in California would be at all. She might as well have rented a house on Bradford Street in Redford's Crossing's most rundown neighborhood. More alarming was that Menzo's assistant, Skye Song, collected their cell phones for safe keeping, effectively sealing them off from the world and any hope of escape.

Her work days in Menzo's salon were long and thankless, and her unsupervised time was limited. Ten hours a day, she shampooed heads and massaged hands for pampered, selfish women who saw her as just another piece of equipment. Their tips were stingy, and any girl who provided less than perfect service was sent for more training, from which they returned with bruised bodies and crushed spirits.

"Do you think it's fair that we're not being paid?" Rochelle had asked Mariah, a pretty blonde from Wisconsin, one day. "I mean, I know we got free training and all, but I worked all day and only cleared twelve dollars in tips."

Mariah's eyes went wide. "Menzo's good to us. We have plenty of food and a place to live," she said, as if reading from a script. Then she turned and hurried to her room. Later that evening, in their shared bathroom, Mariah hissed, "They listen."

The next afternoon Menzo paid Rochelle a visit.

"Do you think we're being unfair to you,

Rochelle?"

Beads of sweat formed on her upper lip. "No."

"We've provided you with valuable training and a career that most girls can only dream of. We've given you a roof over your head and food to eat. We've met your every need, isn't that right?"

She nodded meekly. "Yes, sir."

"When you've paid back the cost of your training and your room and board, you will start to earn a paycheck. I've already explained that to you, have I not? Until then, your tips are yours to keep."

His eyes and tone of voice were stone cold, and she involuntarily shivered.

"Don't forget, you signed an agreement. If you back out of it, there will be legal consequences. Breach of contract is not a small offense. A pretty thing like you, I don't think you'd do very well in prison."

She'd quietly left the room, all of her pretty hopes dashed, knowing without a doubt that she was now Menzo's prisoner. The only thing that kept her going was the hope that one day she would find a way to return home. And now that home had been torn away from her.

Because of another man.

She'd been a fool to trust Sandy, to think

he was different. She only hoped the money Bessie left her would be enough to start over somewhere new. Somewhere far away from Redford's Crossing, where she could forget she'd ever seen Sandy Fairbrother's face.

Sandy left the lawyer's office and after a quick stop home to change into his work clothes, drove out to his current renovation project on Sullivan Street. By the time he arrived, Judge Forrester, his right-hand man and only employee, had finished prepping the downstairs bathroom and was cutting the first sheet of drywall.

"How'd you make out?" Judge asked.

"Fine." He ran a hand over an exposed stud. "Did you get all of the old screws out?"

"Of course I did. I was just thinking about lunch. Have you eaten yet?"

Sandy's stomach revolted at the thought of food. "You go ahead. I'll work on this for a while."

When Judge left, Sandy hung the first sheet of drywall, the weight of Bessie's unread letter on his shoulders and the weight of Rochelle's words on his heart.

You knew we'd find out soon enough so you didn't say a word. That way you didn't have to be the bad guy . . .

He frowned. Did she really have such a

low opinion of him, to think he'd somehow persuaded Bessie to give him her house? Good Lord, he'd rather have stayed invisible to Rochelle than to have her hate him.

He hung a second sheet of drywall, his anger growing. He'd been as stunned by the reading of the will as the rest of them, even more stunned by Rochelle's claim that the house on Orchard Drive was her home. *Since when?* The last he'd known, her home was two-thousand miles away in California. If things had gone wrong for her there, that was certainly no fault or concern of his.

As he prepared to fit the third sheet of drywall into place, he noticed his mistake. He'd measured wrong. The hole he'd cut wouldn't clear the sink pipe. It was a rookie mistake that any other day he would have simply remedied with pipe patch, but today it sent him over the edge. Picking up his hammer, he smashed it into the sheet of drywall, sending broken pieces skittering across the floor.

"Hey, boss, take it easy." Judge stood in the doorway, holding a carry-out bag. "I brought you back a burger. You OK?"

He drew a breath and let it go. "I'm feeling a little stressed out, to be honest, Judge. I think I'll take the rest of the day off."

By the time he picked Jace up from school,

he'd calmed down. They went about their routine; snack, homework papers, a game of catch in the yard. Normally it was Sandy's favorite part of the day, but today Jace's little-boy chatter and his endless questions set Sandy's nerves on edge. The weight of Bess' unread letter and the echo of Rochelle's tearful accusation had him thoroughly gutted.

You turned her against us. Me and Austin both.

She couldn't possibly think that.

But he could see how she might. What had Bess been thinking, leaving her house to him?

Hours later, when the house was quiet and Jace was safely asleep in his room, Sandy carried Bess' letter to the porch to find out.

Dearest Sandy,

   I'm sure you are quite surprised to learn that I have left you the house. As you know, this ol' place meant a lot to me. Carl and I sacrificed and scrimped in the first years of our marriage, living on peanut butter and bread, just to be able to buy it. In it, we sheltered five foster children. Many cups of coffee were shared with friends in this kitchen, games of canasta played, and platters of cookies baked. It's been a place of laughter and love, of hard times and good times, and of much prayer. Within its shelter, I have celebrated births and marriages. I have mourned the loss of family and friends. I survived Carl's time in Vietnam. It served me well for all of these years, but now the house is showing its age, just like this ol' gal.

I don't want Austin to be burdened with it, especially with his first child so close in coming. And I know deep in my heart that the house needs more work than he can afford, if he would hope to get any money out of it. And Rochelle . . . It breaks my heart to finally admit that I will never see my darling Rochelle's face again. She has a new life now, and I'm sure she has no interest in this old house.

I've seen the homes you've restored. The old Edmond House is beautiful again. You are bringing back the town's loveliness, its pride, one house at a time. All of the things we talked about, when I asked what you would do if this house were yours, your ideas for expanding the kitchen and building a little sun porch off the back . . . I hope you will do them now. I love this house, and I love your vision for it. Take it, Sandy. Make something beautiful. Make it fit for a family again. That is all

I ask and more than I could hope for.

Love, Bess

He sat for long moments, letting her words sink in, knowing in his heart that he had no choice except to do as Bess asked. And somehow, he'd find a way to make things right with Rochelle. He couldn't bear her anger and he couldn't lie to himself any longer. She was all he wanted; all he'd ever wanted.

He pulled out his cell phone. Steeling himself, he selected her number. It rang three times before an abrupt shift to voice mail told him his call had been rejected.

Sandy had called her for two days. Rochelle counted eight missed calls on her cell phone. And then he stopped, and his silence was worse than his persistence had been. She missed him.

On Thursday afternoon, she brewed a pot of tea and set out the blueberry muffins she'd baked for Kat's visit. The Hummel figurines, which she'd carefully wrapped and boxed, waited in the living room.

At two o'clock Kat showed up, all hugs and grins, and bulging belly. "I'm so glad we could do this today, Rochelle. I feel like

I may not make it to my due date next week."

"How are you feeling? Any more false labor pains?"

"Just kind of a dull ache. My OB says it's normal." Her gaze swept across the room. "You've gotten quite a bit packed up already. Thanks for doing this for us. Austin's having a hard time with losing Bessie. I don't think he could have faced going through her things, and I'm in no condition to help right now."

"I'm getting through it, little by little. Which reminds me. I came across some things I thought you and Austin might like to have. I put them in Austin's old bedroom."

"I appreciate that."

Kat settled on the sofa, and Rochelle brought in a tray of muffins and tea. There was so much she wanted to discuss with Kat, so many questions she needed answers to. But they were hard questions to ask, and she had no idea where to begin, so she chose a safer topic.

"Kat, speaking of keepsakes, I went up in the attic to look around. It's full of Bessie's Christmas decorations. I thought you and Austin would probably want some of them."

"We'd love to have some of them. I remember the first Christmas that Austin brought me to this house. I couldn't believe all the decorations. It looked like a Christmas store." She laughed. "Or a fairytale land. All those trees glittering with lights. And all those beautiful ornaments Bessie made by hand. I'd never seen anything like it."

"I have an idea for some of those ornaments. Does the town still put up the memorial trees in the park? I thought maybe we could do a tree in Bessie's honor."

"Oh, Ro. I love the idea! And I love you for thinking of it. You know I'll want to help you put it all together."

"I was hoping you'd say that."

"Does this mean you're staying in Redford's Crossing? At least until Christmas?"

"That's kind of my plan."

"I'm so glad to hear that. I was hoping you'd want to be here for the baby's birth, and, you know, for its first few months. I know Austin will be glad, too."

"I'm not so sure about that, Kat." She took a swallow from her teacup. "How is Austin doing?"

"Good days and bad."

"I wish he'd talk to me, but I guess that won't happen any time soon."

"He'll come around eventually."

"Do you really think so?"

"He loves you, Ro. He always has. He's just feeling hurt. He felt as though you turned your back on him and Bessie. If you don't mind me asking, why didn't you ever answer any of his letters?"

She thought of the letters Austin had written her over the years. The earliest ones filled with news of his high school basketball games.

We kicked Eastern's butts all over the court last night. I scored us twelve points by half time. I wish you could have seen it . . .

And later, his well thought out plan for his future.

You know how I've always loved true crime movies? The way the detectives figure everything out, it amazes me. That's what I want to do, Ro. I want to figure out crimes. I'm enrolling in the Criminal Justice program at community college, and after I graduate from there, I'll join the police academy. I'll have to start out as a patrolman, but my goal is to be a detective by the time I'm twenty-five . . .

There was news of the wonderful girl he'd fallen in love with, and then his wedding invitation, and finally his last, brief note:

Bessie is very sick. If you don't come home soon, it will be too late . . .

How could she admit to Kat that she had

been forbidden to come home? Menzo's girls were not allowed to have contact with anyone outside his network. Period. When she caught on that her mail from home was being read, she rented a post office box, sneaking away at every possible opportunity to scribble letters to Bessie. Sneaking away at every opportunity to check for precious mail from home. Waiting for the time when Menzo wouldn't be watching. Nine long years . . .

"I'm sorry, Kat. I'm not ready to talk about it yet. But soon I'll tell you and Austin everything. I promise."

"OK. No problem," she said, but her expression betrayed her disappointment.

They sat in silence for long moments.

"Austin says if the house had to leave the family, he's glad Bessie gave it to Sandy. He's a good guy."

There's no bad guy here . . .

Rochelle absently stirred her coffee. "Obviously his wife didn't think so."

Kat lifted her eyebrows in surprise. "Danielle? She didn't marry Sandy for love."

"She didn't?"

"No. She just wanted to get away."

Ro set her tea on the table beside her. "I'm not sure what you mean."

Kat popped the last of her muffin into her

mouth and daintily wiped her lips. "Danielle already had Jace. When he was a few weeks old, she started dating Sandy, and then they got married. Sandy adopted Jace. And within days, Danielle took off for New York City with some wanna-be hip-hop star, leaving Sandy to raise Jace by himself. Sandy says Jace is a blessing to him, though. He loves that child."

Rochelle gaped at her. "You mean Jace isn't Sandy's son?"

"Not biologically, no. But Sandy's a wonderful father."

"Yes," Ro said softly. "He is."

After Kat left, Rochelle took Bessie's letter down from the mantel. She held it in her hands for a long moment before setting it back in place. Gus scratched at the back door. She removed his diaper and took him outside. Walking around the neglected yard, an incredible sense of sadness and loss welled up inside her. Less than a week ago she'd had thoughts of resurrecting the gardens and repainting the old potting shed. She'd thought it was her property to restore.

But maybe all hope was not lost. After her conversation with Kat, she'd learned that Sandy was a better man than she'd given him credit for. He'd said they could work something out. Maybe he'd allow her to buy the house back from him, to make payments on it, over time.

Back inside, she re-diapered Gus and was pouring a second cup of tea when she was startled by the shrill, persistent ringing of Bessie's telephone. She'd all but forgotten Bessie had a landline, and had not heard it ring since she'd been home. She'd given Kat her new cell number earlier, so it could only be one person calling. Sandy must have decided he had a better chance of getting Rochelle to pick up the house phone than her cell. After taking a moment to collect her thoughts, she picked up the receiver.

"Hello?"

At first, she thought no one was there, but then she heard the sound of soft breathing on the other end.

"Hello?"

The silence suddenly felt sinister. A chill shivered down her spine. She listened for ten seconds more before the caller hung up. Shaken, she replaced the receiver in its cradle. *A telemarketer, or a wrong number, that's all it was.* But then, why hadn't they spoken?

She walked to the table and sat down, trying to think it through. Surely, Menzo hadn't tracked her here. She'd been too careful for that . . .

Rochelle had survived her years in Menzo's employ by being the best. The best hair stylist. The best manicurist. The best makeup artist. Over time she'd become the most requested girl in Menzo's salon. She'd earned the trust of Menzo's salon manager, Skye Song. Knowing that one day that trust would provide her means of escape, she waited.

When Bessie's letters stopped coming, she'd sent a frantic letter to Austin. A week later, she received his two-sentence response.

Bessie is very sick. If you don't come home soon, it will be too late . . .

She'd spent nine years dreaming of her escape, waiting for the perfect opportunity. But now she was out of time. There was only one option and the thought of it scared her to death.

For six months, Skye had left the salon early on Tuesday nights, trusting Rochelle to lock up. She'd had Rochelle cash out the day's receipts and drop the money in the night deposit box at the bank, two blocks away. Rochelle had played out the scenario a dozen times in her head, had planned it down to the last detail.

That night, she made out the receipts as always, put the money in a bank bag, and slipped it in her purse. At nine thirty-five she locked the salon door and walked the two blocks to the bank. With her heart thundering in her chest, she removed the neat bundle of cash from the bank bag before she dropped it into the slot. Then she casually walked around the corner, where a taxi waited.

She directed the driver to the bus station and took the first bus departing California, a ten-fifteen to Reno, Nevada. In Reno, she took a bus to Salt Lake City. In Colorado, she got on a train heading to Nebraska.

Iowa. Illinois. Indiana.

Mile by mile, getting closer to home, $5,000 worth of Menzo's cash in her pocket and an almost crippling fear that each stop would be the end of the line, that Menzo would be there waiting for her.

In Fort Wayne, Indiana, she called Austin from a borrowed phone.

She's gone, Rochelle. There's no point in you coming now . . .

When she finally arrived, tired and heartbroken, at the bus station in Columbus, she took one look at her brother's face and knew he would never forgive her.

And neither would Menzo.

If it were only a matter of the money she'd taken, she'd gladly send it back as soon as her inheritance check from Bessie cleared the bank. But she knew with a sick certainty that it was about much, much more than that. If Menzo had tracked her down, she'd have to leave Redford's Crossing, and soon.

If Menzo had tracked her down, she wouldn't be safe here.

She wouldn't be safe anywhere.

7

On Thursday evening, Sandy drove away from the renovated duplex on Sullivan Street with a sense of satisfaction. The long hours of sweat and frustration he'd put in had paid off. He and Judge were ahead of schedule. He still had the painting and the finishing work to do. But another week and the house would be done and ready to put on the market. Which meant he could start on Dan Williamson's kitchen renovation a week ahead of schedule.

As he drove across town to collect Jace from his grandmother's house, he was thinking about Bessie's house on Orchard Drive. Bob McCormick had told him the official transfer of ownership involved some red tape and might take a few weeks to complete. That was fine with Sandy. Motivated by Bessie's letter, he'd sketched out a few ideas for the house's renovation. He'd knock out a kitchen wall and put in an

114

island, replace the tired, old appliances with new stainless-steel ones, and install larger, more energy efficient windows to take advantage of all the natural light. The bathroom would need a complete gut and update, and he'd add a second half-bath off the master bedroom. But that was all premature until he spoke with Rochelle. He wouldn't proceed until he knew what her plans were. That was what he'd planned to tell her, if she'd taken his calls. Which she hadn't.

He sighed. It wasn't as if he didn't have more than enough other projects to occupy his time. He'd scheduled a light spring in the hope of doing some work around his own place. The big, drafty beast sat on a gorgeous piece of land just outside of town, on a five-acre parcel with a fishing pond, and large, shady trees. But like the shoemaker's barefoot kids, this contractor's home was desperately in need of some tender loving care.

He pulled into the driveway of the small ranch-style home belonging to his ex-mother-in-law and hurried up the walk. She met him at the door.

"I'm sorry to be so late, Sue. I lost track of time."

"Oh, you're fine, honey. I tried to get Jace

to eat some dinner, but he's got it in his noggin that the two of you are getting a pizza tonight." She playfully ruffled the child's hair.

"Can we, Daddy? Can we go to get pizza?"

"We'll see. Now grab your backpack and let's get out of Grandma's hair."

Jace giggled, and when Sue bent to kiss his cheek, he ran his hands through her hair, leaving it thoroughly tousled.

"Oh, you silly boy," she scolded. "What will Grandma do with you?"

Jace giggled and ran out the door. "The last one in the truck is a smelly pair of socks!"

At the Pizza King, Sandy ordered a pepperoni pie. He and Jace went to sit in a booth to wait. Jace was happily chattering about his day at school and the upcoming birthday party he'd been invited to. Sandy did not notice that Carol-Ann Sheridan was there until she stood beside him.

"Hello, stranger."

He grimaced inwardly. How was it that this woman seemed to have a built in GPS that tracked his every move? "Hi, Carol-Ann."

"Pretty day out, isn't it?"

"Sure is. Did Judge remember to stop by and see about that porch light?"

"Yes, he did."

She lingered, and Sandy got the distinct impression in the awkward silence there were words she was bursting to say.

"I'm going to a birthday party! It'll be on Saturday. That's two days from today!" Jace told her gleefully. "It's gonna be a Superhero party, and I get to wear my superhero costume!"

"Oh, how nice for you!" Carol-Ann gushed. "You'll look so handsome in your costume!"

"Uh-huh. I can wear my costume *if* it still fits me, I mean. Dad says I've grown a mile since Poptober."

Carol-Ann laughed too hard and too long.

An uncomfortable itching was starting beneath Sandy's collar.

"So . . . Just the guys tonight?" she asked, a bit too casually.

"Excuse me?"

"My mother heard you were in the restaurant with Rochelle Delany on Sunday night. I just wondered . . ." She left the words hanging in the air.

Sandy grimaced not sure he wanted to answer.

"We went to church," Jace piped up. "And then we got milkshakes. Bessie's daughter is going to make us a chocolate pie!"

"She is?"

"Yep. And a mean macaroni and cheese."

"Well, how nice for you both." Carol-Ann huffed away.

Sandy cringed. That would be a tasty morsel for the town grapevine. He only hoped it was still true.

They finished their pizza and headed home. At the last moment, Sandy took a detour down Orchard Drive, slowing as he passed Bessie's house. It was full-on dark outside now, but there were no lights on in the house. The shades were drawn tight against the windows. The place looked abandoned.

I'll be out tomorrow. Will that be soon enough?

His heart plummeted. Surely, she hadn't been serious?

The brief flutter of a curtain in an upstairs window made him frown. Maybe she'd taken a late nap and hadn't realized the house was getting dark. Or maybe she was ill. Should he check on her, make sure she was all right? After a moment of uncertainty, he continued on down the street.

"Aren't we gonna stop and see Gus?" Jace asked.

"I don't know, Champ. Maybe."

Sandy did not like to text message. His

large hands and big fingers made it frustrating typing on the tiny keypad. But Rochelle refused to return his phone calls, and he wasn't about to drop in on her unannounced again. He nosed his truck to the curb at the end of the block, pulled out his phone, and scrolled through his contacts. When he found Rochelle's name, he opened the message box and painstakingly began to type his message.

Can we talk? Please?

He hit send and waited. Seconds ticked by, and then a full minute. And then two. And then his phone chimed.

Yes.

Five minutes after answering Sandy's text message, Rochelle opened the door to Sandy and Jace.

Jace had a big grin on his face. "We had pizza. Can I see Gus?"

"Of course you can, sweetheart. He's in the kitchen. I've got some chocolate chip cookies on the table. Help yourself if you're not too full."

"I'm not!" Jace scampered past her.

"Just one," Sandy called after him.

As the little boy disappeared into the kitchen, Ro's gaze rested on Sandy. He looked more handsome than ever with his messy hair, a five o'clock shadow peppering his chin. "Come in."

He moved past her and into the hallway.

She shot a hurried glance down the street before closing the door behind him. "Why don't we sit in the living room?" She turned on a lamp.

Sandy perched on the edge of the sofa, seeming ill at ease. He retrieved a folded sheet of paper from his pocket. "Before you say anything, I'd like you to read this." He handed Ro the paper.

As Rochelle unfolded it, the sight of Bessie's lovely, scrolling cursive caused her heart to ache. She read the letter through twice and handed it back to him.

"Bessie used to ask me what I would do with the house if I owned it. I told her all of my grand plans. I thought it was all in fun. I swear to you, Rochelle, I never dreamed she'd leave this house to me."

"I believe you," she said softly. "And I'm sorry for the things I said."

"You were upset. Understandably so."

"That's no excuse. You were obviously very important to Bessie. If I'd been in touch with her, I would have known that."

He tucked the letter back in his pocket. "Bob says it might take a while to get all of the documents in place. I'm fine with you staying here for as long as you need to. I'm sure you have a lot of things to sort through before you go back to California."

"I'm not going back."

His face registered surprise. "You're not?"

"No."

"Not ever?"

"No."

"Oh."

She wasn't prepared to give him an explanation so she stayed silent.

"Well that changes things. Bessie never dreamed you'd want to come back to Redford's Crossing, or I'm sure she would have left the house to you in a heartbeat. When the new deed comes through, I'll sign it back over to you."

The words stole her breath. She was overwhelmed that he would make such a generous offer, ashamed of the terrible accusations she'd made. "You'd really do that? Why?"

"Because it's the right thing to do, that's why."

He was a good man. An honest man and something shifted deep in her heart. "I appreciate that. But I'm not sure I'll be staying in Redford's Crossing, either."

"Where else would you go?"

"I'm not sure."

"I wish you'd stay."

"Why?"

His face colored. "I know I'm no kind of catch, so please don't misunderstand. I was just hoping we could get to know each other a little better."

She would have loved nothing more than to get to know him. But the timing could not have been worse. Her eyes misted. Another opportunity lost.

"What's bothering you, Rochelle?" he asked quietly.

She wanted to trust him, wanted to tell him everything about the secrets that were strangling her. The words ached for release, but she couldn't find a way to say them, and so she told him part of the truth. "Seeing Bessie's letter tonight, reading her words, it was almost like having her back. I haven't read mine yet. I haven't dared."

"I think you'd feel better if you did. There won't be anything hurtful in it. I promise."

"Will you read it to me? Just in case?"

"Do you want me to?"

She walked to the mantel. Her hands trembled as she took down the letter. Taking a breath for courage, she handed it to him.

He unsealed the envelope and took out

the letter. He cleared his throat, and in his deep, rich voice, he read Bessie's words.

My darling girl,
   I remember the night they brought you to me, a lovely, headstrong ten- year-old, with dreams as big as the sky. They warned me that I'd have my hands full with you, and they were right. My hands were full, yes, but how much more, my heart.
   You will never know the joy it gave me to watch you grow up, and to be a part of your journey. I think now of the little girl who danced in my living room, of the teenager who practiced her cheerleading stunts in my backyard, of the lovely young woman I know you have become.
   I hope you are safe, darling. I hope you are happy.
   I have left you my engagement ring. Though not extremely valuable, it is precious to me, and I want you to have it as a keepsake. Perhaps you can have the diamond reset into a necklace that you can wear close to your heart, and maybe you will touch it now and again and think of this ol' gal and smile. That is my hope.
   My prayer is that you will stay close to God, my child. That you will call on Him when times are hard, and that you will find

Him in all of the little pleasures that make up your life. He's there, you know, with you always. And so am I.

Until we meet again, my girl, for now and forever, I love you.

Bessie

The words cut through her, tearing and healing at the same time. Tears fell from her eyes, and a sob escaped her lips. Without a word, Sandy drew near and folded her into his arms. She rested her head against his chest, finding comfort in his embrace and in the strength and solidness, in the *goodness* of him.

All at once, the air around her changed. It pulsed with energy, and an overwhelming peace enveloped her. She recognized it as being the same sensation she'd experienced in church on Sunday, and she knew, without a doubt, that Sandy was praying for her.

"It's OK," he finally said. "Everything will be all right."

And somehow, she believed him.

It had been several moments since he'd heard Jace's sing-song voice drifting through the doorway to the kitchen. Envisioning an empty plate of cookies, he'd have to investigate that situation soon. But first, he would have to end this magical moment.

Lord, not yet.

Not when he'd waited fifteen years for this unspeakable gift; Rochelle Delany in his arms. It was an answered prayer, a dream come true. He was still digesting the news that she wasn't planning to return to California. Something felt off. He could think of several reasons for her decision, none of them pleasant. A failed career? A love gone wrong?

He wished he could take away the sadness of whatever it was that caused her tears. But how? Every single thing he knew and understood about women could fit into a teaspoon. Should he forge ahead, or back off? She said she might leave Redford's Crossing. How could he change her mind?

God, show me what to do . . .

As if hearing his thoughts, she pulled away from him and the magical moment was over.

"I'm sorry."

"Don't be."

"I feel like such a mess."

He'd never seen such a pretty mess. A long, silky lock of hair had escaped her ponytail, and he ached to touch it, to tuck it behind her ear. Instead, he stood. "I'd better go and see what that boy of mine is up to. He's awfully quiet out there, and that's never a good thing."

She smiled, and his world tilted off its axis. And in that moment, he made up his mind. Rochelle wasn't leaving Redford's Crossing. Not if Sandy Fairbrother had anything to say about it.

8

That night, Rochelle drifted off to sleep with sweet dreams of Sandy filling her head. But somewhere in the darkness, Sandy's smile faded and Menzo's face rose up before her, his dark eyes glinting with hatred.

"You've disappointed me, Rochelle..."

The words struck fear like no other in her heart, as they did in the hearts of all of Menzo's girls. Her hands unconsciously groped for the baseball bat she'd left beside the bed.

"You've been talking with that laundry boy again, haven't you?"

Too late, she realized the folly of her actions. She'd lingered for only a moment that morning to chat with Mark, the man from the laundry service who picked up the soiled towels from the salon each week and delivered clean ones. Mark was pleasant and good looking and the conversation was completely harmless. But he was outside of Menzo's network. And for Menzo's girls, talking with him was forbidden.

"What have you got to say for yourself, then?"

She was too afraid to speak, knowing nothing she said would matter anyway. In this trial, Menzo was judge, jury, and executioner.

"You're a foolish, small-minded girl from a foolish, small-minded town. You're nothing, Rochelle. You've always been nothing. Which is why even your own parents didn't want you."

Tears sprang to her eyes, but still she remained silent.

"Have I made you angry?" His eyes smoldered with what looked like contempt. "You have no right to be angry. I've done nothing but look after your every need. I've protected you, delivered you from the nothing you come from. I've been more of a father to you than your own father, isn't that true?"

"Yes, sir," she whispered.

"And this is how you repay my kindness? By betraying my trust?"

His words swam around in her head, confusing her. Was that true? Was she somehow at fault?

"You'd be nothing without me. I'm grooming you for greatness and I simply won't have you settling for someone so mediocre. I don't want you to squander your potential for a laundry worker. I'm offering you the career of a lifetime. I thought you understood that."

She nodded.

"What was it the two of you were discussing?"

They'd talked about a movie Mark had seen the night before, featuring an actor they both enjoyed. Mark had even hinted that he and Rochelle might see a movie together sometime, but she dared not tell Menzo that.

"We just talked about the weather," she whispered, staring at the floor so he would not see the lie in her eyes.

"The weather," he spat. His eyes bored into her, pinning her to the wall. "I've spoken with the boy's supervisor. He won't be bothering you again. And since you've proven yourself unworthy of the home I've given you, you will sleep outside tonight. We'll see how you feel about things in the morning."

His words sent a shock of terror down her spine. The dorm was in a high-crime area of the city. Drug dealers ruled this neighborhood where shootings, stabbings, and robberies were a nightly occurrence. But she'd already made a terrible mistake that morning in chatting with Mark. To argue with Menzo's punishment would be a far deadlier one.

"Help me, God. Please help me . . ." She

cried out in her sleep and awoke bathed in sweat, with Gus nuzzling her cheek. She pulled the baseball bat into the bed with her and stared at the ceiling until she fell back into an uneasy sleep.

When Ro opened her eyes again, sunlight poured through the window. She went to the kitchen, brewed a pot of coffee, then removed Gus' diaper and took him outside. The air was scented with freshly-cut grass. Birds chirped from the treetops and her nightmare life in California suddenly seemed very far away.

Back inside, she poured a cup of coffee and carried it to the window. Sandy's words came back to her.

I know I'm no kind of catch . . .

No kind of catch. Was he kidding?

She hadn't been in a romantic relationship since she left Redford's Crossing nearly ten years before. Menzo did not allow his girls to be in relationships. He did not allow anything in their lives that he could not control. She felt more for Sandy Fairbrother than she should have, after such a short amount of time. She would have loved to see what a month, six months, or even a year would bring for them but it wasn't meant to be. She couldn't seem to shake the feeling that the dream had been a warning. As soon as she received Bessie's inheritance check, she would have to leave Redford's Crossing, maybe head to a large city where she could simply disappear. And this time she wouldn't come back.

It was a beautiful morning.

After dropping Jace off at the elementary school, Sandy went to check on the project on Sullivan Street. With Judge's assurance that he would have the finishing work done that weekend, Sandy met with the realtor to confirm the open house for the following Saturday morning.

"Properties like this one are red-hot right now, Sandy," Kristin Beals told him. "I've sold four properties comparable to yours within the last two months. People want affordable duplexes. If you're sure the Sullivan Street property will be ready, I'd like to do a pre-open house this Tuesday afternoon."

"Do you think that's necessary?" he asked. "We're having an open house on Saturday."

"The more exposure the better. I know that people around town are very interested in seeing what you've done with this house. I'm telling you, Sandy; you're a magician with these old wrecks. That place was a stone's throw away from being condemned, and now it's absolutely stunning. If we have a good pre-showing on Tuesday, we may just end up with more than one offer on Saturday, which gives us a whole lot more negotiating power with the potential buyers. You could feasibly even get more than your asking price."

He was careful not to let the praise go to his head. He'd learned long ago that when it came to real estate there was no such thing as a sure thing. But he had to admit, Kristin's assessment was encouraging. "You're the expert. If you think we need an early showing, then I guess we'll do it."

After the meeting, he drove across town to meet with Dan Williamson. They went over the timeline and the cost of materials and labor for the kitchen renovation in Dan's 200-year-old farmhouse. Dan was more than pleased with the estimate. Everything seemed to be falling into place.

Jace normally spent an hour or two with his grandmother, Sue, after school on Fridays, so with a few unaccustomed free hours to spare, Sandy returned home and headed down to his basement workshop. Maybe he could finish Austin's cradle today.

Small scale furniture had never been Sandy's forte. This was his first attempt at a cradle and he was pleasantly surprised at how well it had turned out. He'd ordered the pattern a month before, when Austin asked him to make the cradle as a surprise gift for Kat. He'd cut the pieces from scraps of sturdy oak he had left over from a previous project. He'd shaped and routed the panels and braces, glued them together and set them with clamps. He'd glued and screwed in the rocker panels and plugged the counter-sink holes, all the while, entertaining pleasant daydreams. Jace was his whole world right now, but Sandy wanted a houseful of kids. He wanted Jace to have a mother and siblings. With the daydreams came a nagging sense of worry. It wasn't too late, not yet. But at thirty years of age, time was definitely not on his side.

He loosened the clamps and lifted the cradle down from the table to inspect it. Seeing the glue had set nicely, he sanded the wood and wiped it clean, then retrieved a can of white paint from the cupboard and brushed a coat on the cradle.

By early afternoon, the second coat of paint had dried. The cradle was nearly finished. But not quite. Austin had told him Kat was decorating the nursery in a baby dinosaur motif and that he would like a dinosaur painted on the footboard, if possible. And that's where the master carpenter was at a loss.

After several attempts doodled on scrap paper, he wadded them and threw them in the waste basket. Jace could have done a better job. Sandy was the first to admit he was no kind of artist. But he knew someone who was.

Upstairs, he made a sandwich and carried it, along with his cell phone, out to the porch. As he ate, a gentle breeze whispered across his face. In the distance, a piece of farm machinery rumbled through his neighbor's field. It was a nearly perfect afternoon. There was one thing that would make it complete and he hoped that would fall into place as well. Wiping his hands on a napkin, he picked up his cell phone and selected Rochelle's number. She answered on the second ring.

"Hello?"

"Good afternoon."

"Hi, Sandy."

"Hey, if you don't have plans this afternoon, there's something here at the house I could use your help with." She didn't answer, so he forged ahead with the half-baked plan he'd put together. "And after that, I thought we could grab Jace from his grandma's and pick up something to eat. You can even bring Gus, if you want to."

Her lengthy pause told him that calling might have been a mistake. He held his breath, glad she could not see the embarrassment he felt coloring his face.

"OK," she finally said.

Surprised relief made him talkative. "Great. You should probably wear old clothes, OK? Why don't I swing by for you in a half hour?"

"Perfect. I'll see you then."

Smiling, he clicked off the call.

Perfect.

Rochelle hung up the phone with mixed feelings. The day had been torture. She'd managed to clean out Bessie's bedroom closet, bagging up most of the clothes for the local thrift store. As if the task weren't emotional enough, she found herself continually drifting to the window, checking up and down the street. Looking for what, she couldn't say.

Russ Swanson mowed his lawn. A mother walked her baby down the block in a stroller. A delivery truck rumbled past, and then a mail truck. All was as it should be, and yet, an uneasy sense of dread seemed to shadow the brilliant April sun. The remnants of her nightmare returned, making her day seem anything but ordinary. She should not encourage Sandy, not when her time here was so short, but his company this afternoon would be a mighty welcome distraction.

He had told her to wear old clothes. She stood in her closet, a wry smile on her face. Old clothes were all she had. She selected a faded gray T-shirt and slipped one of Bessie's old gardening smocks on over top of it. She brushed her hair and pulled it back into a ponytail, brushed on a coat of mascara, and was waiting on the porch when Sandy's truck pulled into the driveway.

Sandy lifted Gus into the backseat and they drove off.

"So what's this project of yours? I'm dying of curiosity."

He grinned. "You'll see."

As the town fell away behind them, she began to relax. They followed the county road for several miles before taking a right-hand turn onto a winding, private drive. She drank in the sight of tall pines and flowering redbuds, a rock wall where a scattering of jonquils and hyacinths dipped their lovely heads, the remnants of some long-ago owner's gardens.

"This is absolutely lovely."

"It was the land that sold me on the place. The house, not so much. Not yet, anyway."

Her gaze swept over the large, unpainted

two-story colonial with its wide, wraparound porch. Two weeping cherry trees stood in full bloom on either side of the front steps. The setting spoke of gentler days when peas were shelled and glasses of lemonade were enjoyed here on summer evenings. The house was a bit rundown, but still absolutely enchanting.

Sandy retrieved a length of rope from his truck, tied Gus to a porch post, and set out a bowl of water. The dog drank thirstily, ignoring a squirrel who scolded him from the treetops. When he'd drunk his fill, he settled onto the grass with a contented sigh.

Inside, the house had the unmistakably disheveled appearance of a home where a man and a little boy lived without a woman's supervision. Toys were strewn across the living room floor while dust bunnies multiplied beneath the furniture. But it was loaded with the kind of charming features that only an old home possessed; a sunny window seat in the dining room, pocket doors, an open staircase, and two stained-glass windows side-by-side on the landing.

"It's got potential, as you can see," he said, as if embarrassed.

"It's fabulous."

"It will be. Someday."

She tucked her hands in the back pockets

of her jeans. "So what is it that you need my help with?"

"Follow me."

He led her down the stairs to the basement and into a full workshop. In the center of a work table sat a baby cradle.

She walked over to inspect it, admiring the beautifully curving headboard, the coat of paint so glossy she could nearly see her reflection. "This is beautiful."

"It's a surprise for Kat. Austin wants a baby dinosaur painted on the footboard. Something cute." He retrieved a wadded paper from the wastebasket, smoothed out the wrinkles, and showed it to her. "As you can see, I'm out of my comfort zone."

The drawing was hideous and she tried not to smile. "Wow."

"Exactly. If I remember correctly, you used to be quite an artist."

She stared at him in surprise. "What makes you think that?"

"Sixth period, senior year. Mrs. McCay's art class?"

A memory of the beloved afternoons with eccentric, bejeweled Sandra McCay came back to her with shocking clarity. "I'd forgotten all about that. You were in that class?"

"Yep. You were the best artist in class.

Remember those prompts Mrs. McCay used to give us, ridiculous things like haunted houses and animal-people, and then say we had fifteen minutes to create them? Yours always looked like professional art. Mine looked like . . . well, like this." He wadded the paper back up and tossed it in the trash.

"I can't believe you remember that." She searched the dusty corners of her mind for a memory of Sandy in Mrs. McCay's art class and could not find one.

"I was hoping you could whip something cute up. I'd like to take the cradle over to them this weekend, if possible."

"Well, I'm a bit rusty, but sure. I'll see what I can do."

She got busy with a pencil and a sheet of paper, and was soon lost in her artwork. She'd forgotten how much she used to enjoy drawing. She'd forgotten how much she used to enjoy so many things. When she was finished with her sketch, a baby triceratops faced a baby pterodactyl, a patchwork quilt heart centered between them. She held up the drawing for Sandy's approval.

"How's this?"

"It's amazing."

"What colors are the nursery?"

"Lavender and mint green. I have some

acrylics here that might work." He retrieved a box of paints from a cabinet and handed it to her. She selected shades of purple and pink, green and blue and began to mix them together. As she transferred the sketch onto the cradle, Sandy stood behind her, watching. She was acutely aware of his nearness and the faint woodsy scent of his aftershave.

"Did you do much painting while you were out in California?"

"No, I didn't."

"I would have thought the ocean would be a pretty inspiring backdrop for an artist."

"I'm not an artist, Sandy. And anyway, I didn't have a lot of free time."

"Oh."

"Do you think this shade of purple is OK?"

"Looks good to me."

As she painstakingly blended the colors onto the sketch, the cartoon dinosaurs came to life, stroke by stroke.

"So what did you like to do, when you did have free time?" he asked.

"Oh, you know. This and that. Can you hand me that rag, please?"

When she'd finished the painting, they left it to dry and headed back to town to collect Jace.

The boy ran to the truck, overjoyed. "You brought Gus!"

"Hi, Jace," Rochelle said, as he climbed into his booster seat.

"Hi, Mrs. Bessie's daughter."

"You can call me Ro, if you want to."

"Can I call you Ro Ro? Like row, row, row your boat?"

She laughed. "Yes, I'd like that."

"I'm hungry."

"What else is new?" Sandy ruffled the boy's hair. "Think we should go and get some burgers?"

"Cheeseburgers! Can Gus and Ro Ro get burgers too?"

"I don't know about Gus, but Ro can, for sure."

They pulled into a fast-food drive through and placed their order, then took their meals back to Sandy's house. As they settled around the table on the back porch, Jace babbled nonstop about his day at school.

Rochelle was grateful for the diversion. It prevented Sandy from asking more questions she did not want to answer about her life in California.

With his meal finished, Jace jumped up from the table. "Can we play Sandy Says?"

"I don't think Ro wants to play that silly game, Champ," Sandy said.

"I love silly games," Ro said, smiling at Jace. "You'll just have to tell me what the rules are."

"I will! It's easy. Come on, Dad."

They moved out into the yard and formed a three-person circle.

"We have to do everything Dad says, but only *if* he says 'Sandy says' first," Jace told her. "If he doesn't say it and you do it anyway, then you lose points. When you get to zero, the game is over."

"How many points do we start with?" she asked.

"I dunno. I think like a thousand."

"How about we start with twenty." Sandy grinned.

He assigned them outrageous tasks. Ro and Jace hopped and leap-frogged and somersaulted and laughed until they cried.

When the game ended, Jace said, "I know! Now let's play Mother May I! Mrs. Ferguson taught it to us at recess."

"Only if I can be the mother," Sandy teased.

"No!" Jace squealed. "You got to be Sandy Says, so Ro Ro's the mother. And we'll be her children."

"OK, children." Rochelle clapped her hands. "The two of you have to back up to that tree at the edge of the pond."

Sandy winked. "You're kind of a bossy mother, aren't you?"

"The tree, mister, or I'll send you back to the storage shed. Jace, you may go first."

"Mother may I take four *giant* steps forward?"

"You may."

"Mother, may I take four giant steps forward too?" Sandy asked.

"No, you may not. But you may take two baby steps backward."

"Doh!"

Jace giggled. "Mother, may I take three bunny hops forward?"

"You may."

They laughed and played until daylight faded and the setting sun glinted on the pond like fairy wands across the water. Rochelle thought how different her life could have been, if only. She'd thought she wanted the excitement and glamour of California, and all the time, all that glittered was right here in front of her. And she'd never even noticed.

In the gathering dusk, Sandy stood dangerously close to her. "My turn," he said. He took three large strides until he stood directly in front of her. "I win."

"You forgot to say 'Mother, May I!'" Jace shrieked. "Now you have to go all the way back to the tree!"

"Awww," Sandy protested.

"You have to, it's the rule! Mother may I take four big froggy hops forward?"

"You may."

On the third hop, Jace reached her and threw his arms around her.

"I won!"

She held him gently, savoring the sweetness of the moment.

"I wish you really were my mother," he whispered.

Her gaze met Sandy's. His stricken expression showed he'd heard what his son had said.

"Can we toast marshmallows?" Jace asked, jumping up and down.

"Not tonight, champ."

"Aww. Why not?"

"It's getting late. We've got to take Gus home and then get you into the bathtub. We'll do marshmallows soon, though."

"With graham crackers and chocolate?"

"Sure."

"Us and Ro Ro and Gus?"

"You bet."

All too soon, Sandy's truck pulled back into the driveway on Orchard Drive. He climbed out and lifted Gus onto the sidewalk. "Thanks again for your help today."

"Thank you for a lovely evening."

"Thank you for a lovely evening, Gus!" Jace shouted from the open truck window.

Sandy smiled his wonderful smile at Ro. "My pleasure."

Gus plodded up the stairs and scratched at the front door. "He looks worn out. I guess I should take him inside and get him diapered for the night."

Sandy laughed softly. "Oh, right."

"You can have him whenever you want to, you know," she said quietly. "Technically, he belongs to Jace now."

"Ahh, maybe we'll hold off on that for a little while yet, if you don't mind."

"I don't mind."

"Good."

"Goodnight, Sandy."

"Good night, Ro Ro."

Inside, she locked the door and watched from the window as Sandy drove away. It had been a magical day. The best day she could remember in a very long time. Breaking the spell, she moved to the kitchen and checked the answering machine. The red light was steady. There were no messages, no missed calls. Relief washed over her and she scolded herself for her foolish fears. She had let her imagination run away with her. Everything was fine. Menzo Maricello wouldn't find her here. He wouldn't even try.

9

The day with Rochelle was so pleasurable and at the same time, it caused so much pain. Sandy brushed a coat of clear polyurethane on the cradle. While it dried, he set about cleaning up his workshop. He washed his brushes and hung his tools back on the peg board. He wiped the wood shavings from his table and shook the cloth into the trash bin. If things went as planned, he and Rochelle would be delivering the cradle to Austin and Kat tomorrow. He could hardly wait to be with her again.

And he couldn't stop thinking about all that had happened the day before. He relived each moment — the fast food picnic on the porch; he, Rochelle and Jace laughing and playing in the yard while Gus watched from under the trees. Jace throwing his arms around Rochelle after Sandy let him win that silly game.

I wish you really were my mother . . .

The images made him smile. But they also broke his heart, these mirages of the life he wanted so badly to have. The life he'd dreamed of on the day he bought this big old house, and every day since then. The one that included a family; a mother for Jace, and a companion for himself. A woman like Rochelle.

No, not a woman *like* Rochelle. He wanted Rochelle.

He'd always wanted Rochelle.

He swept a pile of sawdust from the floor and dumped it in the wastebasket. At seven years old, Jace had begun to notice that his friends and classmates had mothers. He'd started to ask Sandy hard questions about his own motherless state. Sandy was at a loss for what to tell him. The truth was Jace's mother had walked away when he was a newborn and never once looked back. He couldn't tell his son that. But then, what could he tell him?

The cellar door opened.

Jace called down the stairs. "Daddy, can I have Fruity Puffs for breakfast?"

"I left them on the counter for you, along with your bowl and a spoon. I'll be up in a minute to help you do the milk."

"I can do the milk myself."

"Are you sure? It's a full gallon."

"Yep, I'm sure."

The door closed, and his son's footsteps moved around in the kitchen above him. Sandy sighed. Jace was getting to an age where he wanted more independence and Sandy was having trouble letting go. The years were speeding by. Before he knew it, the day would come when his boy would ask for the keys to his car. The day would come when Sandy would no longer be needed. He supposed every father struggled to balance encouraging his son's independence with the overwhelming urge to keep him tucked safely under his wing.

It was that protective instinct that kept Sandy single. He'd gone on a handful of dates over the years, but had never brought any woman home to meet his son. It had never felt right. Until last night. Rochelle's presence here had been so natural and so incredible. It had him wanting things he had no business wanting. She'd made it clear that she wasn't interested in getting to know him, and that she had no plans to stay in Redford's Crossing. It would be wise for him to back away before Jace started wanting her, too.

He thought again of the impulsive hug Jace had given her, saw again the pure, unmasked longing in the boy's eyes. Those were the images that broke Sandy's heart. Problem was he didn't know how to not want her, or how to help Jace not want her when they both obviously did.

God, I need Your help. I need You to show me how to be a good father. Show me how to be enough for my child --

Upstairs he heard a thud, and then the sound of scampering footsteps before the cellar door opened again.

"Daddy, can you come up?"

"What's wrong?"

"I spilled the milk."

His prayer answered, if only for a moment, Sandy laughed and headed up the stairs.

The sunlight streaming through her window had Rochelle out of bed and out the door, determined in her mission. Armed with a rake, a pair of garden gloves, and a roll of trash bags, she set to work bringing order to Bessie's flower beds. As she carefully removed the decaying leaves and the garbage that had collected in the front garden, the tender shoots of hyacinth and daffodils became visible, and she had a sudden memory of her first spring with Bessie and how they had planted flower bulbs together.

"Careful, child. These little ladies are tenacious, but if you dig the holes too deep they'll

have a long journey to find the sun . . ."

"What's tenacious, Bessie?"

The woman had smiled. "You, my darling girl. You are tenacious!"

The sunshine on her face seemed like a smile from heaven. The act of clearing away old debris and pulling stubborn weeds was therapeutic, almost spiritual, as she felt the cleansing power of her past mistakes being purged from her soul.

"Good morning, Rochelle. Isn't it a beautiful day?" Jan Swanson made a bee line across the yard.

"Yes, it certainly is."

"I'm so happy to see you tending Bessie's flower beds. I've wanted to come over and weed them so many times, but I wasn't sure it was my place to."

"I hate that the beds got this bad," Rochelle said. "Bessie sure loved her flowers."

"Oh, that she did." Jan rested her arms on the picket fence that separated their properties. "I have so many wonderful memories of time spent out here with her. I learned so much from her. I treasure the things in my own garden that she shared with me; a bulb, a slip of periwinkle. She always said beauty was meant to be shared. Of course, I never had the green thumb that Bess did. That woman could make a clump of buttercups look like a work of art." She gazed lovingly across the yard. "What are your plans for the house, if you don't mind me asking?"

"Ahh, I'm really not sure yet."

"I know it's none of my business, dear, but I couldn't help notice that the Fairbrother boy has been here several times since you've been home. That made me and Russ wonder if you and Austin had plans to sell him the place."

"I'm sure you can see that the house needs a lot of work. Austin asked Sandy to come by and take a look, maybe give us an estimate. Wait right there, Mrs. Swanson, while I go and get your pie plate for you. The pot pie was amazing, by the way!"

She hurried to the house, hoping to buy a few moments to collect her thoughts. She was under no obligation to tell Jan Swanson anything, yet she hated to be rude. Jan and Russ had always been kind to her and they had been very good neighbors to Bessie. And by now, half the town probably knew about Bessie leaving the house to Sandy in her will.

Thankfully, when she returned to the yard, she was able to distract Jan by also giving her the stained-glass nutcracker ornament.

"Thank you so much, honey," she said,

clutching the decoration close to her heart. "It's just the sort of thing I had in mind. I'll treasure it for the rest of my life."

Jan's talk turned to Russ' recent doctor visit and her concerns for his health. When Jan finally headed home, Rochelle returned her garden tools to the shed and went inside to get cleaned up. After a shower and a cold drink, she put in a call to her sister-in-law.

"How's everything going, Kat?"

"So far, so good, I think. Austin's getting off work early today. We're having an ultrasound. Hopefully it'll be our last."

"How exciting. Nothing's wrong though, is it?"

"Not at all. They just want to get an idea of how much baby I have in here," Kat said. Rochelle pictured her lovingly caressing her tummy. "Then they'll decide how much longer I get to be pregnant. I hope it won't be too awful long."

"I hope not, too. Hey, I was wondering if you'll be home tomorrow."

Kat laughed. "As far as we know. Why do you ask?"

"Sandy and I might stop by for a little while, if that's OK."

"Really? Sure, we'd love that."

"OK, good. I'll get back to you with a time

once I've talked to Sandy. Have a great day, Kat."

She ended the call with a smile, knowing she'd left Kat with a hundred unanswered questions. Opening her closet, she put on one more of the many T-shirts she'd collected, along with an ancient pair of jeans. Ro checked her look in the full-length mirror. She could not go on dressing as if she were sixteen years old. Enough was enough. It was time to buy some new clothes.

She and Sandy were planning to deliver the baby cradle tomorrow. Rochelle decided to pick up a baby blanket and possibly a plush stuffed dinosaur to go with it. Between that and new clothes, the decision meant a trip to the plaza.

The changes Main Street had undergone in her absence surprised her.

The greasy spoons that had lined the second block were now trendy coffee bars, cupcake shops and sweeteries. Goodman's Department Store, which had been the jewel of the third block, was now a senior citizen's center. Most of the clothing and shoe stores had either closed for good or relocated to the new plaza outside of town. She'd noticed a baby store out there, as well as several clothing outlets. She frowned. It would be crowded on a Saturday, though, and likely, a repeat of her trip to the grocery store. She could drive thirty minutes to Chillicothe, where no one would know her, but that would be risky without a driver's license. She'd just have to brave the plaza. Maybe a pair of dark sunglasses would help disguise her.

Her thoughts turned to the baby and she smiled wistfully. There were so many things she wanted to give Austin's child. Mostly, she wanted to give of herself. She wanted to be the very best auntie she could be, especially considering she'd probably never have a child of her own.

The memory of Jace's impulsive hug last night and his hopeful words caused a strange stirring in her heart. She'd never thought much about having kids one way or the other, but being there with Jace and Sandy, spending the evening with them had felt as if she had come home. That like her long-ago daffodils, after a long, exhausting journey, she'd finally found the sun.

The parking lot of the shopping plaza was only half full when she arrived, not nearly as crowded as she'd expected for a Saturday afternoon. Even so, she drove to a far corner of the lot and nudged Bessie's car into a parking spot. There were plenty of spots that were closer to the baby store, but with a borrowed car and no driver's license, let alone auto insurance, she wasn't taking any chances.

She found a clothing outlet that looked promising and went inside. The prices were high, but she still had plenty of Menzo's money in her pocket. An hour later, she left the store with two shopping bags full of slacks, skirts, and summer tops. She popped into a lingerie store next, purchased some new underclothes, and walked out with a sense of satisfaction. She'd forgotten the simple pleasure of picking out her own clothes. Menzo had provided what he wanted his girls to wear, most of it too short, too tight, or too impractical to be comfortable. She was learning to think for herself again, and it felt wonderful.

Shading her eyes with her hand, she scanned the length of the plaza. The baby store was close enough to walk to, but farther than she wanted to carry three heavy bags full of clothes. She'd stow her goodies in the car and then walk back to the baby store.

She strolled towards Bessie's vehicle. The car still sat alone at end of the lot, except for a large, black SUV that had parked right beside it. "Are you kidding me," she murmured, slightly irritated. "You had the whole parking lot, mister."

As she drew nearer to the SUV, her mind subconsciously registered its familiar license plate; a white background with navy blue letters, a splash of red cursive at the top that spelled the name of its state.

California.

"You're a long way from home, mister." She stood for a moment, uneasily clutching her shopping bags, a sense of wrongness swirling in her gut. A California license plate in Redford's Crossing, Ohio. What were the odds of that?

Unless it wasn't a coincidence.

Surely, Menzo hadn't set one of his goons to bring her back.

She was being silly, of course she was. But unable to ignore the warning sirens that shrieked in her head, she turned around and headed back toward the plaza.

Behind her, a car door opened, and then slammed shut.

"Miss?" a male voice called out and she quickened her pace. She heard his footsteps coming up quickly behind her. Her heart pounded and the icy fingers of fear clawed at her insides.

Oh, please, God . . .

Should she scream?

A hundred yards away she could see people moving around outside the stores. She was too far away to be heard and too far away to be clearly seen. She didn't know how close she could get to them before the man overtook her. The only thing she knew for certain was that he would never get her in that truck. Not alive, anyway.

Oh God! Oh, God, I need you!

The pounding of footsteps was closer now. She squeezed her eyes shut, a prayer shrieking in her head.

Please, God. Father in heave . . . Please save me.

10

The temperature had risen ten degrees in the thirty minutes that had passed since Sandy zipped Jace into his costume. The birthday party was an outside event, and he hoped the boy wouldn't get overheated. He unbuckled Jace's booster seat and helped his son from the truck.

"You behave yourself today, OK?"

"I will."

"I put a pair of shorts in your bag. If you get too hot, you can change into them."

"I know."

"Be sure to thank Mrs. Simpson for inviting you."

"Dad, you already told me that."

"Just making sure." He reached for the bag containing a change of clothes and the birthday gift Jace had sloppily wrapped two nights before. "Here, don't forget Dakota's birthday present."

"Thanks."

"Are you sure you don't want me to walk you up to the door?"

"No, I can go by myself."

"OK." He hesitated briefly before giving the boy a kiss on the top of his head. "Have fun, champ."

"I will!"

Jace skipped up to the front door and rang the doorbell. When Jolene Simpson opened it, Sandy gave her a quick wave.

"Afternoon, Jolene."

"Hey, Sandy!" she called.

"Beautiful day for a party."

"I couldn't have asked for better weather. Especially considering the festivities are being held in the back yard!"

"Well, you have fun with that. I'll be back for him around four o'clock."

"No hurry. He can stay as long as he wants." She ushered Jace inside and the door closed behind them.

Sandy climbed into his truck. Reluctant to leave, he watched as a miniature male superhero stepped up to the front door, followed by an equally small female superhero. Ignoring the all too familiar pang of regret, he put his truck in gear and drove away. What was wrong with him lately? It would be good for Jace to spend a Saturday with kids his own age, instead of running errands with him. Sandy would just have to get used to the idea that his son was growing up, that he had discovered other friends.

Sandy thought about that for a moment. Even as a child, he had never seen his father as a hero. That title had been reserved for his older brother, Joe. Their father had been someone to fear and to obey, but not to adore. How many times had Joe stepped in and confessed to mistakes he had not made in order to save Sandy from their father's wrath? Too many to count, Sandy realized. Sometimes, in moments of quiet reflection, Sandy wondered if their father had ever regretted his heavy handedness with his sons. If he'd ever loved them at all.

Thank You, heavenly Father, for showing me what a father should be.

Back home, he wandered down to his workshop. The cradle had dried to a glossy sheen. It was good to go and he wondered if Rochelle had remembered to call Austin. In case she'd forgotten, he went upstairs and made the call.

"Sandy, good afternoon!"

"Hey, Austin. Did Rochelle get ahold of you?"

"No, but she talked to Kat earlier."

"OK, good. I've got the cradle all finished for you. I thought we might bring it by tomorrow, if that's convenient."

"That works for me. Thanks for getting it done so quickly."

"No problem. Is early afternoon good?"

"It should be." He laughed softly. "Unless the baby has other plans."

"Oh, right."

There was an awkward silence before Austin said, "Sandy, the thing is, are you and my sister, like, seeing each other now?"

The question caught him off guard. "What? No. I just needed her help with painting the dinosaurs on the cradle. I thought she might like to be there when you gave it to Kat."

"OK, good."

Good?

"Would it be a problem for you if we were seeing each other?"

"No, not for me. But maybe for you."

The conversation had taken an unexpected turn for which Sandy was not prepared. He was searching for an appropriate response when Austin said, "Look, I know it's none of my business, but be careful. My sister's not very stable."

Sandy's anger sparked and he fought to control it. "I don't know, Austin, she seems pretty sound to me."

"What I mean is . . . she's not dependable. With relationships. I just don't want to see anyone get hurt."

"Well, I'm a big boy. I can take care of myself."

"Listen, I've got to go. Kat's got an appointment. We'll see you tomorrow afternoon. Thanks again, brother."

Sandy was only too happy to end the call. Families had disagreements. He understood that. But he wished Austin would ease up. Rochelle was gone for a long time, yes, but she was home now. And she was trying to repair her relationships. Sandy would do everything in his power to see that she stayed in Redford's Crossing. He wished Austin would do the same.

Bess Casey had led her foster children by example. She'd taught them to pray by praying with them and in front of them. Some of her requests were small and simple. Others were outrageous. Rochelle had learned from years of observing Bessie's prayer life that sometimes God answered prayers in his own good time. Other times He stepped in immediately.

Father God, save me!

The prayer shrieked in her brain as she hurried across the parking lot. As if she was living her worst nightmare, the plaza seemed to grow farther away, and the footsteps behind her, ever closer with every step she took.

She heard a vehicle roll up behind her at the same moment a man's voice called her name. "Rochelle Delany!"

She screamed.

The footsteps behind her stopped.

"Rochelle?"

A cappuccino-colored sedan had pulled to a stop beside her, its passenger-side window down. She shot a disbelieving glance at the sky, and then at the driver, who looked at her with concern.

"Chad?"

"Doggone, it is you. I heard you were back in town. How've you been, girl? It's sure been a long time."

She'd dated Chad Chaplan briefly in her senior year. He'd been handsome as all get out, but he was arrogant and self-centered. Rochelle found his constant bragging to be a bore and the romance hadn't lasted beyond their second date. He was the last person Rochelle had wanted to run into when she returned to Redford's Crossing, but at that moment, he looked like a knight in shining armor. A God-send.

"How's life in California treatin' ya?" he asked.

She was acutely aware of the man behind her. His frustration and indecision seemed to hang in the humid air.

"It's been forever! I have so much to tell you, Chad. Let me buy you a cup of coffee."

"Well, I was actually just on my way to —"

She flung open the passenger door, threw her bags in the back seat, and slid inside. Chad gaped at her in disbelief.

"Actually, Ro, the thing is —"

She put up the window and clicked the lock. "Chad, go."

"What?"

"Step on the gas. Now!"

With a glance in his rearview mirror, Chad seemed to catch on. He pressed his foot on the gas pedal and the sedan shot away from the man, across the plaza, and out of the parking lot. By the time they turned onto the county road, Rochelle was trembling uncontrollably.

"Are you OK?" he asked.

She fought for air. "I don't know."

"Who was that guy? Was he stalking you?"

"I don't know who he was, Chad. Can you please take me to police station?"

"Sure thing."

Within moments, they reached the city

limits. Chad drove down Main Street and pulled in the Redford's Crossing PD parking lot.

"Do you want me to go in with you?"

"No, I'll be fine. I just need to talk to Austin." She reached into the back seat and retrieved her shopping bags. "Thanks. You probably just saved my life."

"Hey." His hand lightly grazed hers. "If you need anything at all while you're in town, you know you can call me, right?"

"Thanks, Chad," she said, sliding from the car. "I appreciate that."

As the sedan pulled from the lot she took a moment to calm herself. She'd planned to tell Austin the truth about her life in California in her own way and in her own time. Now that wouldn't be possible. She'd have to tell him today and she wasn't at all prepared. She desperately needed his help. She only hoped he'd be willing to listen to her.

Inside the police department, she was intercepted by a plain clothes officer. "You look lost," he said with a smile. "Can I point you in the right direction?"

"Yes, thank you. My name is Rochelle Delany."

His smile grew wider. "Rochelle, of course. Austin mentioned you were back in town. I'm Joe Cooper, his partner. Is there something I can do for you?"

"Would it be possible for me to speak with Austin for a moment?"

"Well, it would be, except that he left here about a half hour ago to take his wife to an appointment. Is there anything I can help you with?"

Her heart sank. In the confusion, she'd forgotten all about Kat's ultrasound. "No, I'll catch up with him later. Thank you, though."

Outside, she shot hurried glances up and down the street. The SUV was nowhere in sight.

What now?

She could walk the few blocks home, but that would make her an easy target if the man was watching her. She should have asked Chad to wait. What could she do?

Think, Rochelle!

Not knowing who else to call, she ducked around the corner under an ancient maple tree, and pulled out her cell phone. With hands that wouldn't stop shaking, she selected Sandy's number, praying the call would not go to voicemail. It didn't.

"Hey, Ro, what's up?" Sandy asked.

"Sandy, I need your help."

"What's wrong?"

"I'm at the police station. Can you come and pick me up?"

"Of course I can. Is everything all right?"

"Yes and no. I'll explain when you get here. Can you come right now?"

"I'm on my way."

Fifteen minutes later Sandy's truck pulled into the lot. She hurried over to it and climbed inside, stowing her bags in the backseat. "Thanks for coming."

"Good Lord, Ro, you're as white as paper. What happened?"

"I don't want to talk here." She shot a nervous glance down the street. "Can we go to your house?"

Thankfully, Sandy didn't ask any more questions. As the truck rolled out of town, she plopped down the sun shade. Thankfully, it had a mirror in it. She checked for any sign of the black SUV behind them. It wasn't until she was safely inside Sandy's house that she allowed herself to relax. Sandy directed her to the living room and brought her a cold glass of iced tea, then sat on the couch beside her.

"Thank you." Her hands trembled as she took a swallow from her glass. Her gaze wandered around the room. "Where's Jace?"

"He's at a birthday party."

"Oh, good."

He watched her for long moments, waiting patiently as she struggled to find the right words. "Thank you for coming to get me. I know I'm acting very strangely. I had . . . a scare."

"What kind of a scare?"

"A man tried to abduct me at the plaza today."

"What?"

"I went to pick up a gift for the baby, and some new clothes for myself." She indicated the shopping bags she'd dumped on the floor. "When I came out of the clothing store a dark SUV was parked right beside me, even though I was at the farthest end of the lot. I had a gut feeling something was wrong, so I turned and headed back. Then a man got out of the SUV and started to follow me. I had to leave Bessie's car there. Chad Chaplan happened to come along, and I kind of carjacked him into taking me to the police station, and . . ." her voice cracked as she rambled on. "I prayed to God, and He saved me, there's no other way to explain it. I honestly don't know what I would have done if Chad hadn't driven up."

"I'm thankful he did. I don't even want to think about what might have happened." He took her hands in his, and she saw both concern and anger in his eyes. "You hear of this happening more and more often, even in small towns. I never dreamed it would happen in Redford's Crossing. What did the cops say?"

She lowered her gaze. "I didn't tell them."

His angry expression turned to one of disbelief. "Rochelle, why not?"

She fell silent. She didn't want the entire Redford's Crossing Police Department, let alone Sandy, to know the truth about her life in California. But now there was no way she could keep her secret.

"Because what happened today is only a very small part of the story, Sandy. There's a lot more that you don't know. I wanted to tell it to Austin, first."

"Please tell it to me," he said softly.

Her phone chimed. As she retrieved it from her bag, her hands trembled so violently the phone slipped through her fingers and fell to the sofa.

Sandy picked it up and checked the screen. "It's Austin."

"Can you put it on speaker, please?"

He did so and set the phone on the coffee table.

"Hello, Austin," she said.

"Rochelle, what's going on?" her brother demanded.

"Why do you ask?"

"Joe Cooper said you stopped by the station looking for me earlier. He also said Chad Chaplan's spreading it all over town that he saved you from being abducted in the plaza today. Joe said the phone lines at the police station are blowing up right now."

She buried her face in her hands. "Word travels fast."

"People are scared. This is Redford's Crossing. In case you didn't remember, things like this don't happen here. If that's what really happened."

His anger was more than she could bear. Tears filled her eyes. "I stopped by the station because I wanted to talk to you about it. I forgot about Kat's appointment."

"So it did really happen?"

"For heaven's sakes, Austin, do you think I'd make something like that up?"

"I would hope not."

"Look, I don't want to discuss this over the phone."

"Then we'll come over. We're just finishing up here."

"She's with me, and she's extremely shaken up," Sandy said. "We're at my house. You're welcome to come, but I'll thank you to leave the attitude at the door."

"Understood," Austin said, then ended the call.

Sandy reached for the phone and disconnected the call on Rochelle's end.

"I'm sorry," she said.

"What are you sorry for?"

"For putting you in the middle of another family feud."

He took her hand again. "I know he's your brother, and I probably overstepped. But you're the victim here. No one should be disrespectful to you. Not even your brother. Not in this house."

What seemed mere moments later, she heard tires crunching on gravel as Austin's car pulled into the driveway.

Sandy opened the door.

Kat hurried to Rochelle and drew her into a hug. "Thank God you're all right." She stood back and studied her face. "You are all right, aren't you?"

"Yes, I'm all right, but what about you? What did the doctor say?"

"Everything's good. Looks like I'll be in this condition for at least another week."

"You look so tired. Please, sit." Ro indicated the spot on the couch where she'd been sitting. "I'm so sorry to add more to your plate."

"Don't be silly. And don't mind Austin," Kat said softly. "He was really scared when Joe called and told us what he'd heard. He just doesn't know how to show it."

Rochelle had a sudden flashback to when she was twelve years old. She was practicing cartwheels in the backyard while Austin played with his trucks at the picnic table. After three successful turns, she'd attempted a fourth and come down hard on a jagged rock. It had sliced through her hand and the gash bled profusely. Crying, Austin ran to the house to alert Bessie. Once the cut had been cleaned and bandaged, Austin would not speak to Ro for the rest of the evening.

"I don't know why he's so mad. I'm the one who got hurt, not him."

Bessie sat on the edge of her bed and tucked a strand of hair behind Rochelle's ear. "He was scared, child. He saw all the blood, and you lying on the ground like a broken doll. You're everything to that little boy. I think he can't bear the thought that he might ever lose you."

Ro snapped back to the present when she heard murmured voices in the foyer.

Austin entered the room, followed by Sandy.

"Come sit down, babe," Kat said, patting the space beside her on the couch.

As Austin took his place beside his wife, Rochelle searched her brother's eyes for a trace of that little boy. Only the intent gaze of a police detective stared back at her.

"OK, Ro. Tell us what happened," he said. "Start at the beginning and don't leave anything out."

His expression went from intent to alarmed as she recounted her experience at the plaza.

"Have you ever seen the guy before?" he asked.

"I didn't get a good look at him, but no. I'm pretty sure I haven't."

"And you have no idea who he was?"

Her gaze briefly met Sandy's and then fell away. The shame of her past was almost more than she could bear. What would Sandy think of her once he knew? What would any of them think of her? "I don't know who he was. But I'm pretty sure I know who sent him."

"Whoa, wait. You think someone sent the guy to abduct you? Who would do that?"

Her mouth went dry. She took another swallow of tea. "Someone who wants revenge."

"But who could want revenge against you?" Kat exclaimed.

"Someone in California," she whispered. "The SUV had California plates."

"It must be something pretty serious, for

someone to come all that way to seek revenge," Austin said, his expression unreadable. "Why don't you tell us everything that happened?"

A small sob escaped her lips. "I don't know where to start."

"Take your time," Austin said.

Sandy moved to her side and laid a gentle hand on her shoulder. "Just start wherever you feel comfortable."

"You can tell us, Ro," Kat said. "We're here for you. We're your family."

As she glanced from one beloved face to another, the kindness she saw gave her the courage, at last, to tell them everything.

11

"I had a lot of reasons for leaving here nine years ago, but none of them had a thing to do with you or Bessie. I hope you know that, Austin. I loved you both dearly."

Austin's slight nod of acknowledgment gave her the courage to continue.

"It was just . . . I was twenty-one years old, and I felt as if life was passing me by. Redford's Crossing seemed like too small a town to contain all of my big dreams. So when I saw the ad offering an exciting new life in California, I thought it was the answer to all of my prayers. Bessie tried to tell me that anything that seems too good to be true probably is, but my mind was made up. I swallowed the lies hook, line, and sinker like the naïve child I was. I didn't know then that the Internet was a hunting ground for predators."

"Predators?" Kat asked.

"Yes." She reached for her glass and took

a swallow of tea.

The room was silent as they waited for her to continue.

"When I got to Sunny Springs I was interviewed by a man named Menzo Maricello. After the interview, he said I had been accepted into the stylist's program, and he offered to train me for a position in his salon. He promised me the life I'd dreamed of and I was over the moon. I thought he was a suave and successful businessman, with his hotel and his salon, even a small-time movie company. But they were all just fronts for labor trafficking. And worse."

"What do you mean?" Austin asked.

"I mean, after a few days of training, after he handed us bogus cosmetologist's certificates, the other girls and I were forced to work in Menzo's salon for free until we'd paid back the cost of our training. But no matter how hard we worked, and no matter how many hours we put in, it was never enough. We were never square with him. I'd signed a contract without even reading it. I had no way of knowing I'd made a deal with the devil. Menzo threatened to have me arrested if I breached the agreement, and I believed he could legally do that."

"That's debt bondage," Austin said, his expression incredulous.

"Yes."

"My God, Ro. Why didn't you ask us for help? We would have come and gotten you. We'd have found a way."

"At first I was too ashamed. And then I was too afraid."

"You couldn't just leave?" Kat asked. "Go to the police and tell them what was going on?"

"Menzo didn't allow us to have phones, or ID, or freedom of any kind. I'm sure my Ohio driver's license expired years ago."

Austin gave her a sharp look, but then kept writing in his notebook.

Rochelle went on, "He kept us broke, working long hours in the salon during the day, and imprisoned in our own home at night."

A dark shadow crossed Sandy's face. "What do you mean, imprisoned?"

"The neighborhood we lived in was not a safe place, to say the least. As young women it would have been suicide for us to even walk down the street after dark, let alone try and find our way to the police station."

"That's horrible," Kat said. "I'm so sorry that happened to you, Ro. And here everyone thought you were living a dream life."

"To our clients at the salon, or to anyone else, there didn't appear to be anything unusual about us at all. We were just a group of young girls trying to earn a living. No one knew what was really going on. And we were too afraid of Menzo to speak up."

"He hid you in plain sight," Austin said.

"I'm so sorry, Ro," Kat said again. "What an awful man."

"He made his money from the sweat of our labor, but worse than that, he hijacked our minds, made us feel as if he was the answer to all of our problems and that we were indebted to him. He twisted the facts, made us believe we were wrong in our thinking. If any of his girls dared to question his authority, they disappeared. Eventually, though, we all disappeared, a little more with each page torn from the calendar until there was nothing left of us except what Menzo wanted us to be."

"I wish I could get my hands on him," Sandy said quietly.

"Year after year, I held onto the hope that someday I would find a way to escape. I did manage to get a post office box, because someone read all our mail. That was my one tiny bit of freedom, and I could only check it if I was sent on an errand to the post office. Menzo never let down his guard. When I got Austin's note that Bessie was running out of time, I knew that come what may, I'd have to take my chances. Menzo's assistant, Skye, had started trusting me to lock up the salon at night and deposit the day's receipts in the night deposit box at the bank. One night I took the money and ran. I ran for home. And now he's found me." She broke down then.

Sandy gently massaged her shoulders. "It'll be all right, Ro. You're not alone anymore."

"You're safe now," Kat soothed.

"I stole money."

Austin's pen hovered above his notepad. "I'll need the names and addresses of Menzo's hotel and salon, as well as the address of the house you lived in, and the names and descriptions of any girls who were there with you. Chances are pretty good that most of them are either illegal aliens or runaways. Tell me as many specifics as you can, Ro."

"What will you do?"

"First I'll collect all the information I can. And then I'll talk to my captain and see how he wants to proceed with this."

"But what can a little police department in Southern Ohio do about a labor trafficking ring in California, babe?" Kat asked.

"For starters we can recommend an investigation, based on information the Sunny Springs Police Department may not have.

And if it was one of Menzo's men who came after Ro today, they've crossed state lines. That makes it the FBI's business."

An icy fist gripped Rochelle's heart. "You mean there would be a federal investigation?"

"Human trafficking is a serious crime. The feds have more resources than a local police department ever will. I'm sure they'll want to get involved."

"There's something else you should know." She stared down at her hands, shame burning her face. "I modeled for some of Menzo's ads to try and entice young girls to come work for him. Skye said that made me Menzo's business partner. She said that if I ever opened my mouth, I'd be going to jail right along with him."

Sandy squeezed her shoulders. "You weren't his partner. You were his prisoner."

Austin sighed. "We'll sort all that out later. You were coerced, that couldn't be more clear. But for now, I don't think it's safe for you to stay at Bessie's house. The guy is probably lurking somewhere in the shadows, waiting for another chance to grab you. I feel as if you should come and stay at the house with us."

"We can make up the couch," Kat offered. "It's not fancy, but I think you would be comfortable."

"If they know about Bessie, then they can connect her to you as well," Sandy said. "They might come looking for her at your house. No one can connect her to me. I think she should stay here."

"You could be right about that," Austin said. "What do you think, Ro?"

"It's awfully sweet of you, Sandy, but what about your safety, and Jace's?"

"I can take care of myself, and my son."

"People might get the wrong idea, with me staying here. You know how Redford's Crossing is. It would destroy your reputation."

"Not if nobody knew you were here."

"That would be the key," Austin said. "No one can know she's here. It's the only way to keep everyone safe. Sandy, you'd have to stick very closely to your usual routine, come and go as you normally do, and tell no one."

"You can count on it."

"OK, good. I'll send a couple of guys by the plaza with a cruiser this evening and have them drive the car back to Bessie's house. Our friend in the SUV may be still watching it. If the cops go, it'll just look like normal police business. We're just retrieving an abandoned car."

As Rochelle handed him the car keys she had a sudden, sinking thought. "What about Gus?"

"I'll get him," Sandy said. "We'll bring him back here."

"I don't want you anywhere near Bessie's house, Sandy," Austin said. "I don't want to give anyone a reason to follow you back here. We'll have to put Gus in the kennel for the time being."

"Absolutely not!" Kat said.

"Babe . . ."

"He wouldn't understand that and he'd feel abandoned. It would break his heart. He can stay right at the house with us."

"He'll be an awful lot of work for you, Kat," Rochelle said. "With the diapering and all."

"Don't be silly. I don't mind changing Gus' diapers. It'll be good practice for me."

"Are you sure, babe?" Austin asked.

"Of course I'm sure."

"OK." Austin turned to Rochelle. "I'll be in touch after I've talked with the captain. In the meantime, don't leave this house."

"I won't."

"And any time Sandy's not at home, don't answer the door for anyone but me. I'll let you know ahead of time if I'm coming by."

"Got it."

"I'm so glad you're safe now, Ro." Kat hugged her hard. "I'll pray every day that you stay that way until that awful man is behind bars."

The icy fist of fear slowly began to melt, replaced by a feeling of warmth she'd long forgotten; a treasure she'd somehow lost that was found again. The love of her family.

When Austin's car pulled from the driveway, Sandy stood at the window for a long moment before he closed the blinds.

"What are you thinking right now?" she finally asked.

He turned to face her. "I'm thinking you deserved a much better deal than the one you got. And I'm still thinking I'd love to get my hands on Menzo."

"You don't think I deserved what I got, for running off like I did?"

"People grow up and leave home all the time, it's no sin. You were young, and he was slick. You can't blame yourself for being a victim." He sighed. "To be honest, I'm kind of blaming myself. At least for part of it."

The comment stunned her. "Why would you blame yourself, Sandy? You had nothing to do with it."

"All those nights Bess and I talked about

you. She kept saying she knew something was wrong, that she knew you'd be in contact with her if you could. She was convinced you were in some kind of trouble. I wish I'd taken her seriously. I wish I'd done something to help you."

"What could you have done?"

"I don't know." He shrugged. "Something."

"You're doing something now. And I appreciate it more than you know. I just hate the thought that I might be putting you and Jace in danger."

"I can take care of myself, Ro." His eyes shined with grim determination. "And I'll protect you and Jace with my life."

His phone chimed, breaking the tension of the moment. He pulled it out of his pocket and checked the screen.

He pecked at an icon on his screen and put the phone to his ear. "Gosh, I'm sorry Jolene, I got in the middle of something and lost track of time. I'll be there in a few minutes . . . No, I'd rather he came home tonight, but thanks . . . OK, I'll be there shortly." He ended the call. "I have to pick up Jace from the birthday party. I guess it would be best if you stayed here."

"OK."

"I'm a hundred percent sure that no one

followed us. But like Austin said, don't answer the door and stay away from the windows. I'll be back in thirty minutes at the most."

She nodded.

"Are you sure you're OK?"

She attempted a smile. "I'm sure."

He went to her and enveloped her in a warm, safe embrace. "We'll get through this."

She was shipwrecked, and he offered a life raft. Her arms tightened around him and she held on for dear life.

12

The next morning the unmistakable aroma of brewing coffee pulled Rochelle from her sleep. Sandy had insisted on sleeping on the couch, offering Rochelle his bed. She'd slept more deeply last night than she had in longer than she could remember. Opening her eyes, she gazed around the unfamiliar room. It was definitely a man's room, the plain white walls bare of artwork, the furniture consisting only of a bed, an unmatched dresser and night stand, and an oversized leather chair whose shabbiness was no doubt forgiven due to its comfort. But brilliant sunlight flooded in through a large picture window, making the room feel airy and inviting.

Irresistibly drawn by the wash of sunshine, she moved to the window and looked out at the gnarled old apple tree where a pair of robins hopped busily from branch to branch as they added bits of dried grass to their nest. A tire swing drifted lazily back and forth in the morning breeze. It looked like an old-fashioned folk painting, and she was suddenly overcome by a sense of well-being. It had been a very long time since she'd felt so safe.

Voices hummed downstairs; Jace's high pitched chattering followed by Sandy's lower tones. Padding down the hallway to the bathroom, she smiled. What would it be like to wake up here every morning? To belong here?

Recognizing that those were dangerous thoughts, she pushed them away. She splashed water on her face. An unopened pack of toothbrushes sat on the counter, next to a new comb in a different package. She opened the packs, brushed her teeth using the toothpaste tucked in a holder, and then combed her hair. Ready for the day, she headed downstairs to the kitchen.

The room was in chaos. She smiled from the doorway as Jace slapped a spoonful of peanut butter between two slices of bread, knocking a package of cookies to the floor. Gobs of grape jelly dotted the table and countertop. Noticing her in the doorway, he broke off his chattering and rushed to hug her.

"Ro Ro! Daddy said we're supposed to be

quiet and let you sleep but I'm glad you got up. We're making a picnic!"

"That sounds like fun." Her gaze swept over the mess. "What are you putting in your picnic?"

"Peanut butter and jelly sandwiches, potato chips, pickles, and chocolate chip cookies!"

"Wow, that's quite a feast."

"It is, but we need a lot of food 'cause we're going fishing for the whole day. You, me, and Dad."

She shot Sandy a glance, eyebrows raised. "We are?"

Sandy grinned, looking hopelessly boyish in a pair of cartoon pajama bottoms, his hair disheveled from sleep. "Help yourself to some coffee. Jace, remember how I said grown-ups need a few minutes of peace and quiet in the morning? Let's try not to ambush Ro the minute she gets up, OK?"

"What's ambush mean?"

"It means to jump out at someone when they're not expecting it."

"He's fine." Rochelle poured a cup of coffee and then added a splash of milk and a spoonful of sugar. "I'd like to hear more about this fishing trip."

"There's a little inlet off the pond out back. It's very private. I thought it might be a nice place to spend the day, if you want to join us. I started stocking it a couple of years ago and now there's more wide-mouth bass in there than ten people could eat. I thought we might have a fish fry, later."

"That sounds nice." She reached for a slice of toast and buttered it.

Sandy handed her the jar of grape jelly.

Jace had moved to the table, and he bounced up and down on his chair. "I'll show you how to catch 'em. It's easy. You don't even have to do the worms. Dad can do it for ya."

"In that case, count me in."

After breakfast, she changed into one of the new pairs of jeans she'd bought and a pale blue top. Sandy gave her an old pair of wading boots to wear and they set off for the pond, armed with fishing poles, tackle box, a picnic basket, and an empty pail for the fish they planned to catch.

The fishing hole was in a quiet little cove surrounded by pine trees. She hadn't expected it to be so lovely. A sense of peace and safety returned.

Sandy retrieved a jar of worms and baited each of their hooks.

"Look at the size of those worms!" she exclaimed.

"I dug 'em up myself," Jace told her

proudly. "They're called night crawlers, but I get 'em in the morning. I get the big ones 'cause they're the kind the fish like best."

"You dug up all of these worms yourself? Good job."

"Shhh. You gotta be quiet," he whispered as they settled on the bank. "Dad says the fish won't bite if they hear a lot of jabbering."

She and Sandy exchanged smiles.

"OK, thank you for telling me," she whispered.

Rochelle had never fished before and didn't expect to enjoy it, but when she felt the first tell-tale tug on her line she could barely contain her excitement. "Sandy, I think I've got one!"

"Well, look at you, getting the first catch of the day!" He helped her reel in the fish, then removed it from the hook and dropped it in the bucket with a splash. "That one's definitely a keeper."

"You did it, Ro Ro! I told you the fish like my worms!" Jace shouted. He snuggled in beside her. The sweet warmth of him prompted her to thank God for the gift of this child and his father.

By early afternoon, their bucket was full. After they'd eaten their picnic lunch, Jace ran off to chase grasshoppers in the tall grass beside the pond.

"He's so adorable," she commented.

"Yeah, he is. He can be a handful, though."

"I think it's wonderful that you spend time to teach him things. It's the little things he'll remember."

"I hope so. I'm trying to give him a better childhood than I had. My father never took us fishing. He never took us much of anywhere."

She could relate all too well. Bessie had spent years undoing the emotional damage Ro and Austin had endured, and had set about filling their childhood with special moments, what she called the little things.

"How'd you turn out so good, without having a role model?" she asked, genuinely curious.

"I had a role model. It just wasn't my father."

"Who was it then?" She gazed at him with interest.

"Believe it or not, it was Coach."

"Coach MacNamara?"

"Yep. Coach Mac took me under his wing, taught me how to play the game."

"Football."

"Life." He looked out across the cove. "He taught me the value of hard work, of trying my best, and of being satisfied, win or lose, as long as I gave it my all."

"Good advice."

"More than that, he told me about the youth group at his church and encouraged me to go. I met God there. I honestly don't know what would have become of me, if not for Coach Mac."

She smiled. "Saved by grace and football."

"Yes, ma'am. That's about the size of it."

After a time, their talk turned to the house on Sullivan Street Sandy had recently renovated.

"That house has been a dump for as long as I can remember," she said.

"The project was a bear, I won't lie. We got into a mess with the plumbing. I'll be glad to sell this one and be done with it."

"You love what you do, though, fixing up these old houses."

"I like the satisfaction of having fixed them more than the actual fixing," he said. "There's something about bringing order out of chaos that's just . . . soul satisfying."

"I get it. That's kind of the way I feel when I've given someone a really nice haircut. Like in some small way I've helped someone to be better than they were."

He smiled. "Same idea, different canvas. Have you thought about contacting Vanessa

Green at the homeless shelter? I'm sure there are some gals there who could use a pick me up."

"That's a really good idea. Maybe I'll do that, when things are a little more . . . normal."

Their conversation was easy and natural. She could sit right there on the creek bank and talk with him forever. It was a wonderful day, and would have been perfect if not for the dark threat of danger Menzo had cast over it.

She hadn't taken her cell phone to the pond, hadn't wanted the distraction. When they arrived back at the house, she discovered she'd missed two phone calls from Austin. She carried her phone to the porch and returned his calls.

"Where were you all day?" he asked.

"We went fishing. Don't worry, we didn't leave the property."

"OK, good."

"What's up?"

"I had an interesting conversation with Tim Braggs from the Sunny Springs PD last night, and another one this morning."

Her stomach clenched. "You did?"

"It seems they've had their eyes on our friend for a while now. They have reason to believe he runs a prostitution ring out of his hotel."

"That wouldn't surprise me a bit."

"He's pretty slick, I'll give him that. Looks as if we can add money laundering to his list of skills. Of course, none of the hotel employees will talk to the cops."

"They're too afraid of what Menzo would do to them."

"I get that. What's more alarming is that they sent an undercover officer in a couple of weeks ago. She seems to have disappeared."

The familiar fist of terror squeezed Ro's stomach until she felt ill. Knowing full well how Menzo handled people who crossed him, she greatly feared for that officer.

"They weren't aware of Menzo's ties to the salon you worked in, though. They're checking into Skye Song. What you've told us gives them probable cause to ask a judge for a search warrant for the place. They could have that as early as tomorrow."

The words stole her breath.

"I'll keep you updated as I get new info. Just stay out of sight, OK?"

"I will. Thanks, Austin."

She ended the call, her earlier happiness evaporating as she thought about the hornet's nest she'd stirred up. It was all happening so quickly. She could only imagine Menzo's fury when he found out about the search warrant. She took deep breaths, willing her racing pulse to slow down. In nine years, she'd never known anyone to cross Menzo Maricello and live to tell about it.

Sandy was no kind of master chef, but fish fries were definitely his specialty. He'd breaded and fried the bass to golden perfection. He'd whipped the mashed potatoes until they were as light and fluffy as clouds, and his coleslaw was a work of art. Rochelle barely touched any of it. He shot glances at her as she moved the food around on her plate. The joy he'd seen in her eyes earlier seemed to have vaporized like the morning fog. Something about her phone call to Austin had upset her; that was clear. He'd have given anything to find out what it was.

"I don't need a bath before church," Jace announced, breaking into Sandy's thoughts. "I can just go like this, right?"

Sandy sighed. Whether or not to go to church this evening was something he'd battled with all day. He felt uneasy about leaving Rochelle alone for the evening, but Austin had made it clear he was to stick to his normal routine. Sunday evening church service was a big part of that routine. If he and Jace didn't show up people were bound to notice.

"You think it'd be OK to go dirty and stinky like that? To God's house?"

Jace's shoulders slumped. "No."

"Then get moving."

Rochelle watched the exchange, a hint of a smile on her lips. "You've got to give him credit for trying."

"He's fine once he gets in the tub. He just hates the thought of it."

"Typical little boy. Austin was the same way as a kid."

"You won't be afraid to be here alone, will you? We could stay home tonight."

"Of course you won't stay home. I'll be fine."

"If you're sure."

"I'm sure."

He carried his plate to the sink. "Is anything wrong? You seem a little quiet tonight."

She hesitated for long enough that he wasn't sure she'd tell him. Finally she said, "Austin says the Sunny Springs cops have been investigating Menzo for weeks and not getting anywhere. Now that they know about his ties to the salon, they may be able to make some progress."

"That's good, right?"

"Yes, it's good."

"But?"

"An undercover agent who was working in his hotel has disappeared. I can only imagine what happened to her."

He sighed.

"It's just . . . Over the years there were some girls who tried to stand up for themselves. Others tried to run away. They all disappeared, too. I wish I'd had the courage to speak up a long time ago."

"Why, so you could disappear, too? He's a monster, Ro. You can't blame yourself for that."

"I don't know if I'll ever not feel guilty." Tears gathered in her eyes.

Sandy did the only thing he could think of. Returning to the table, he took both of her hands in his and bowed his head. "Father in heaven, please help Your child, Rochelle. Open her eyes so she can see how valuable she is to You. Open her mind so she can understand Your gift of forgiveness, and open her heart so she can feel the power of Your great love."

They sat in silent prayer for a moment, then she squeezed his hand and let go. "Thank you."

"My pleasure."

After his shower, Sandy changed and

reluctantly steered Jace toward the front door. "We won't be more than a couple of hours."

"I'll be fine."

"I'll call you when the service ends and let you know when we're on our way home."

"All right."

When they arrived at the church, Sandy cautioned Jace one last time. "We're not telling anyone Ro Ro is staying at our house, remember? It's a secret."

"I know."

"It's really important, Champ. OK?"

"Dad, I *know*."

That night's sermon was about perseverance. About knowing what was true and having the courage, against all odds, to pursue it. Sandy's thoughts wandered back over the lovely day he, Rochelle, and Jace had spent together, and knew in his heart that she was his truth. From that long-ago day on the football field when she'd spontaneously kissed him, he'd known, as much as a mixed-up teenage boy could know, that they were meant to be together. Why hadn't he had the courage to pursue her?

His thoughts drifted back to Mrs. McCay's art class. He'd admired Rochelle's artwork, but he'd never once told her so. And all of those visits he'd made to Wally's

Corner Market when she was a cashier there. The endless candy bars he'd bought, but hadn't even wanted, just to be where she was. Why had he never asked her out? All those years of loving her from afar, and he'd let her go off to California without a fight. What ate him up the most, though, was not taking Bessie's concerns seriously. He'd wrongly assumed Rochelle had forgotten all about Redford's Crossing; out of sight, out of mind. He'd never dreamed her life was the nightmare he now knew it to be. He should have at least spoken with Austin. If Austin had made the call to the California police department three, two, or even one year ago, it might have spared Rochelle some of the guilt and pain she was feeling now.

When the service ended, Sandy was anxious to get home, but Jace would be expecting their Sunday night milkshakes at Maddy's. It was another part of their routine and he dared not detour from it. In the church parking lot, he took a moment to check in with Rochelle.

"Everything all right there?"

"Right as rain."

"Good. We're going to Maddy's to grab a couple of milkshakes. Do you want one?"

"Heck, yeah."

"We'll see you in about a half hour then."

The balmy evening had brought out half the city. Most of the tables at Maddy's were occupied, including his and Jace's favorite booth. Sandy greeted several friends and neighbors, then steered Jace to the counter to place their order; two strawberry milkshakes and two chocolates. He heard Rochelle's name spoken more than once.

People were still buzzing over yesterday's events at the plaza.

"And nobody's seen her since?"

"This town is getting as bad as the city. Poor Rochelle!"

"Where could she have gone off to, I wonder?"

He squeezed Jace's hand as a reminder to keep quiet.

"Hey, Sandy," Bill Swensen, a former classmate of his, called from across the diner. "The old duplex on Sullivan Street is looking good. Have you got it up for sale yet?"

"Not officially."

"I'd sure love to see what you've done with the inside," Bill's wife, Loren, chimed in.

"It doesn't even look like the same house," someone else added. "That wraparound porch you put on made it a showplace."

"We're having a pre-showing on Tuesday from three to six. It'll be a sneak preview. You're more than welcome to come out and have a look."

Several murmurs went through the room that encouraged Sandy he'd done the right thing for the place. He hated the open houses that went along with his renovation business but saw them as a necessary evil. He hadn't loved the idea of doing two open houses for the Sullivan Street property, but maybe Kristin was right, and he would have a solid offer before the official open house on Saturday even took place.

"You're all set, Sandy." Maxine Potter set the milkshakes on the counter and totaled the sale. "It'll be sixteen dollars."

He handed her a twenty and told her to keep the change, then propelled Jace out the door. They'd barely reached the truck when a woman called after him.

"Excuse me, sir?"

He turned.

The woman walked toward him. She was strikingly beautiful, her long, caramel colored hair streaked with blonde, and her skin the dewy, sun kissed hue of a fashion model's. As she reached him, he noticed that her eyes were a stunning shade of violet, one that he was sure did not occur naturally. Some kind of colored contact lenses, must be.

"What can I do for you?" he asked.

"I'm sorry to bother you. I couldn't help overhearing about your open house. I'm new in town and am looking to invest in a duplex. If the price is right, I might be interested in buying your property." She smiled, revealing a set of perfect, white teeth.

"Great. It's number two-eighty-eight Sullivan Street, first left turn after the railroad tracks, if you want to check it out." He gave her the price that he and Kristin had set. "I'll have to stay pretty close to that."

"That might be doable. I really like the area. Everyone seems so friendly here."

"Where are you from?" he asked, genuinely curious.

"Michigan."

He laughed. "And you dare to say that out loud?"

She looked puzzled, almost insulted. "Michigan's not so bad."

"No, I mean . . ." He indicated his hoodie emblazoned with the college name.

She gave him a polite smile. "Oh. Right."

"So what brings you to Redford's Crossing?"

"A job transfer to the hospital here. I'm a

nurse practitioner. But I'm looking to buy a duplex as a second income. Figure I can live in half and rent the other half out, let the rent money pay the mortgage. I could save a good chunk of my salary that way."

"That sounds like a sound plan."

"This seems like a nice place to settle down, maybe raise a family someday. And a place to get really amazing milkshakes." She smiled at Jace. "You must really like them."

"I do."

"Do you always get two?"

"We got four," Jace informed her. "One for me, one for dad, one for Ro Ro, and . . . Dad, who's the other one for?"

Sandy grimaced inside. "For later."

"I'm sure Ro Ro will love his milkshake," the woman said. "Is that your dog?"

"No!" Jace squealed. "She's our friend."

"You're a goofball," Sandy ruffled Jace's hair, and quickly lifted him into the truck. When he'd buckled him in his booster seat and shut the door, he turned back to the woman. "Ro Ro is my son's *imaginary* friend. She's also his very clever way of getting a second milkshake."

The woman laughed. "Gotcha."

He climbed into the driver's seat. "So I guess I'll see you on Tuesday."

"Three to six, right?"

"Yep."

"And you'll be there the whole time? I'd really rather deal with the owner than a realtor."

"Yes, I'll be there."

"Great. I'll see you at three o'clock on Tuesday then."

Sandy pulled out of the parking lot with mixed feelings. Overall, he felt positive about the open house and the interest it was already generating. He sighed. As for Jace's blunder, he thought he'd covered that pretty well. He'd have to caution the boy again, but he didn't think any damage had been done.

13

On Monday morning, Rochelle awoke before the sun came up. She lay in bed, listening to the unfamiliar sounds of the house — the various creaks and groans as the old walls and floor boards settled, the hum of the refrigerator, the popping of the water heater. She'd gone to sleep last night listening to the sound of rain on the roof and thinking about Sandy's prayer. It stayed with her throughout the night and was her first waking thought.

Help her to see how valuable she is to You . . .

It had been a long time since she'd felt anything close to valuable. Her years of growing up in Bessie's house were the closest she'd ever come to that. Bessie had showered her and Austin with love and affection, but even so, deep down, being abandoned by her parents had damaged her self-esteem. She'd spent her teenage years working hard to prove her worth. To herself, and everyone else.

And then came adulthood, with Menzo chipping away at her confidence day after day, telling her she was nothing. Menzo. The very thought of the man turned her stomach inside out. Menzo had valued her only for the money she could bring into the salon.

Could it really be true that God could love her unconditionally? Could anyone?

She wasn't certain how much time had passed when she heard the shower running, and then the clinking of silverware, and Jace's high-pitched giggling, followed by Sandy's murmured responses. She lay still, savoring every moment of it. No one had dared talk very much in the dorm, knowing their every word was being listened to and evaluated. She hadn't realized how much she'd missed the sound of human voices, the sounds of home. She hadn't realized just how solitary her life had become. She was enjoying being here more than she should, and that frightened her. Over the years, she'd learned not to want anything too badly. If you didn't want for things, it hurt less to have them taken away.

Finally, she heard the front door close, Sandy's truck started, and gravel crunched under the tires as he drove out of the driveway. She made her way downstairs to the kitchen and saw a note propped beside her place at the table.

Good morning. The coffee's fresh. We saved you some breakfast, but help yourself to anything in the fridge that looks good to you. See you tonight.

Sandy

Smiling, she opened the fridge. A plate of bacon and eggs waited on the top shelf. She popped it in the microwave, then poured a cup of coffee, and, after the oven chimed, carried it all to the back porch. The bacon was beyond burned, and the eggs were almost rubbery, but she could not remember when she'd enjoyed breakfast more. It had rained all through the night and the colors of the grass and the newly budded trees were vibrant, the stillness of the morning broken only by the volley of birdsong echoing through the valley. How could she doubt that God loved her, when He'd brought her to this wonderful place?

After a second cup of coffee, she carried her mug to the sink. A greasy fry pan stared at her, charred bits of bacon clinging to its sides. Underneath that pan was another, this one crusted with scrambled eggs. Cups and plates littered the countertops. She rolled up her sleeves, ran the sink full of water, and squirted in some dish soap. If she was freeloading, the least she could do was be useful.

With the dishes drying beside the sink, she swept the floor and wiped down the countertops, then opened the cupboards and took inventory. Graham crackers. Chocolate pudding. In the fridge, she found a container of whipped topping and some butter. She smiled. This would be the perfect day to make the chocolate pie she'd promised Jace.

After a hot shower, she rummaged through the clothes she'd bought and changed into a pair of jeans and a T-shirt. She tidied Sandy's bathroom and made the bed.

Moving to Jace's room, she straightened the sheets and blankets on both the top and bottom bunks and picked up the clothes that were strewn across the floor. Beside his pajama pants was a rumpled shirt many sizes too big for him. Holding it up, her breath caught. She hadn't seen one in years. Turning it over, the number 54 jumped out, and just above, the name "Fairbrother" was written in bold red letters across the black fabric. Sandy's football jersey. Back in the day, it was the most coveted piece of clothing at Redford's Crossing High School. And now it had been relegated to a little boy's pajama top. It sparked a feeling deep inside, but Ro couldn't name it. She folded the jersey and pajama bottoms and put them on Jace's pillow.

She found furniture polish and a dust cloth in the utility room closet and went to tackle the living room.

As she dusted the coffee and end tables, a sudden memory surfaced. It was the Monday after the playoff game in her sophomore or junior year. The victory had been astounding and everyone's spirits were high. That Monday any girl who was anyone donned a player's jersey in school. Every girl but Rochelle. She'd dated the star quarterback, Max Patterson, since the beginning of the school year. After a silly argument she couldn't even remember now, they'd broken up the day before the big game. There had been an announcement in homeroom that morning that the coaches were throwing a pizza party at Maddy's Diner to celebrate the football team's victory. Anyone who showed up wearing a jersey got a free milkshake.

The first period bell rang, and she scooped her books up from her desk. "I guess I'll be paying for my own milkshake," she said, loud enough for Teddy Holmes, an unbearably cute defensive lineman to hear. "Since I don't have a jersey to wear now."

"Do you want to wear mine?" a soft voice asked behind her.

She turned. One of the linemen watched her intently. He wasn't first string, or even second. She didn't even know his name.

"Nah, I'm good," she said. Just before she turned away, she saw something in the boy's eyes. A curious mix of anger and embarrassment. He had visibly translated *I'm good* to mean *I'm too good.*

In her mind's eye, Rochelle suddenly saw that Sandy had been that boy she hadn't valued enough to wear his jersey. Back then, he'd held her in high esteem, even though she was not always nice. The realization was sobering.

By late afternoon, the house was clean, and her chocolate pie was made. She'd just slid it into the refrigerator when her phone chimed. She glanced at the screen, and hurriedly accepted the call.

"What's up, Austin?"

"A lot. It looks as if things are moving pretty fast out in Sunny Springs," her brother told her. "The judge signed off on the warrant for the salon last night. Early this morning the police seized all of the employees' W-2 forms and social security records. It doesn't look good for our friend. As we suspected, most of his employees are either illegal immigrants or underage runaways."

She gripped the back of a chair. "So what happens now?"

"Well, they wanted to bring Skye Song in for questioning but nobody seems to know where she is. They're looking for her now."

The knot of dread tightened in her stomach as she thought of what Menzo might have done when he discovered that Rochelle and his money had disappeared on Skye's watch.

"Anyway, it turns out the salon employees weren't any more forthcoming than those at the hotel. Half of them don't even speak English." He hesitated. "Ro, they'll probably need you to come forward."

Her knees went weak, and the knot in her stomach suddenly felt like a noose around her neck. "What do you mean, come forward?"

"I mean, sit down with them. Tell them everything you know. Sign a written statement. Testify at a trial, if it comes to that."

"I don't know if I can do that."

"It might be the only way to put Menzo away. To save those poor girls in his salon, and Lord knows how many others."

She pushed out a shaky breath.

"It's your decision, but I think you should, and I know you can. You're one of the bravest people I know."

She disconnected the call and sank into a chair. She didn't feel very brave at all. In fact, she was scared to death.

At four o'clock Sandy and Jace strolled through the candy aisle at the store.

"We're getting gummy worms?" Jace asked.

"Ro called and asked me to bring some home. She said she needs them."

"What for?"

"To eat, I would imagine. She also says she has a surprise for you."

Jace's eyes went wide. "What kind of surprise?"

"You'll have to wait and see."

Jace grabbed a bag of candy bars from the shelf. "I think she needs these, too."

Sandy smiled. When his call home went to voicemail earlier that day, it took everything he had not to leave the job site and run home to check on her. She'd finally returned his call an hour ago, explaining she'd been on the phone with Austin. She asked him to bring home gummy worms, but she wouldn't tell him why. He was so relieved to hear her voice he would have agreed to bring the entire candy aisle, if she'd asked him to.

Walking in the front door a half hour later, he smelled the unmistakable aroma of comfort food simmering in the kitchen. The living room was spotless. Following his nose, he discovered Rochelle at the stove, stirring a saucepan of what looked like barbequed hamburger. The sight cased a deep longing to swell inside his heart.

"Are sloppy Joes OK?" she asked.

"Sloppy Joes are our favorite."

"Sloppy Joes!" Jace grinned and thrust the shopping bag at her. "We got the gummy worms for ya."

"Good. Thank you."

"Dad said you have a surprise for me."

"I do."

"Can I have it?"

"Not until after dinner."

"OK." Jace's brows knit. "Are we going fishing? 'Cause you can't use those kinda worms."

She laughed, a soft, jingle bells sound that melted Sandy's heart. She leaned down to cradle Jace's face in her hands. "No sweetie, the gummy worms are not for fishing."

When Jace went to wash up for dinner, she removed a chocolate pie from the fridge and strategically arranged the candy on top. "Mud pie, complete with worms," she explained. "Bessie used to make it for Austin from time to time. It was one of those *little things* of hers I was telling you about."

"I'm sure Jace will love it." He wanted to say more. So much more. Instead, he took the safe strategy. "I should probably get cleaned up." By the time he'd showered and returned to the kitchen, a light rain had begun to fall.

They carried their plates to the porch and ate their Sloppy Joes amid a soothing symphony of raindrops.

"How was work today?" she asked him. "You're doing a kitchen remodel, right?"

"Yep. We made a good start, busted up some old cabinets, knocked down a wall. You know, man stuff."

"Sounds like fun."

"Demo day usually is."

He told her about his plans for the new pantry, the recessed lighting, the new granite countertops, and the farm house sink. She asked questions and really listened when he answered, and he wished again that it could always be like this; sharing his thoughts at the end of the day with someone other than a seven-year-old.

"Are people saying much around town?"

she finally asked. "About me, I mean?"

He hesitated and then admitted, "A good bit, yes."

"So I'm the talk of the town." She sighed. "What else is new?"

"People are concerned, Ro. And they're pretty outraged over what happened at the plaza. You're one of ours."

He saw the doubtful expression on her face and wondered how it was possible that she didn't know how much the town still admired her, how proud they were of her. "People here care about you, Rochelle. They always have."

"I wasn't always very nice back in school, was I?"

He shrugged. "You were just a kid."

"I'm just a kid," Jace interjected.

"A little kid with big ears," Sandy said, tweaking his son's ear.

"Can I have another piece of pie?"

"No, you can go wash your hands, and then do your school papers while I wash the dishes. After that, maybe we can play a game of Crazy Eights."

Jace skipped off to the bathroom pumping his fist, delighted with the promise of a game after homework.

Sandy and Rochelle gathered the dirty plates and carried them to the kitchen. He filled the sink with water and squirted in some dish soap. "Thanks for making dinner."

"It's the least I can do. But if I'm doing the cooking I'll have to send you to the store with a proper grocery list."

"Why? What's wrong with hot dogs and canned spaghetti?"

She gave him a playful shove and he returned it. As they washed and dried the dishes, she grew silent.

"Everything OK?" he asked.

"I might have to go back to California and testify against Menzo." She lifted her gaze. Terror rose in her expression. "None of the girls who work for him will talk. Austin says my testimony might be the only way to put him in jail where he belongs. Even so . . . I'm scared, Sandy."

"I'll go with you."

"Would you?"

He cradled her face in his hands, much as she'd done earlier to Jace. "He won't hurt you again. Not on my watch." Gazing into her eyes, everything inside him wanted to kiss her. Instead, he released her, picked up a dish towel and swiped at the counters. "I've always wanted to go to California anyway. Maybe after you take care of your court business we could see the redwood forest. That's one of the things on my bucket list."

"Redwoods aside, you'd really go with me?"

"Sure."

"Why would you do that for me?"

Looking in her eyes, there was nothing in the world he would not do for her. He wanted to say as much, to tell her how he felt, how he'd always felt. Instead, he took the safe road again and told half of the truth.

"Because you're my friend."

Lying in bed that night, Rochelle thought about friendship and about love. She treasured Sandy's friendship, but she wanted their relationship to be so much more than that. She'd once had that chance, and she'd thrown it away. Oh, how she wished she could travel back in time and rewrite her story.

As her eyelids grew heavy, thoughts of Sandy merged with troubling fears of Skye Song. Why couldn't the police find her? Skye was obsessively possessive of the salon. Rochelle could not remember a single time in nine years that Skye hadn't reported to work. What could have happened to her? With conflicting emotions swirling in her head, she fell into a fitful sleep . . .

It was unusual for Menzo to visit the dorm. When his car pulled in that night, all the girls scattered to their rooms. Moments later, Rochelle was summoned to the kitchen, where Menzo and Sky waited. Neither looked happy.

"Where did you go today on your lunch break, Rochelle?" Menzo asked.

Her mouth went dry. "It was such a pretty day out; I . . . I went for a walk."

"I see. And where did you walk to? Anywhere special?"

She could see that he already knew. Lying to Menzo would be a worse mistake than the one she'd already made.

"I stopped at the post office."

"For what reason?"

"I wanted to mail a letter to my brother."

"So you weren't just out for a walk, after all. Your route was intentional."

"Yes."

"And what was this letter about?"

"It was a birthday card."

Menzo was silent for a long moment as he digested the information.

"He's my brother," she said meekly.

"We're your family now. I thought you understood that."

"I do."

"And yet you sneak off to mail cards to people who don't care a single thing about you. This isn't the first time you've visited the post office, is it, Rochelle?"

Her heart pounded. Menzo's girls were not allowed to roam the city un-chaperoned. She'd been careful, but obviously not careful enough. Head down, she stared at the cracks in the linoleum. "No, sir."

"How many other times have you been there?"

At least a dozen, but she dared not tell him that. "Twice."

"Two other times, besides today? When you told Skye you were out for a walk?"

"Yes, sir."

Eyes cast downward, she heard him remove his belt, and she braced herself.

"Skye, come here."

Ro watched in disbelief as three times he laid the belt across Skye's back while Skye stood tall and unflinching. Blood seeped through her shirt.

"You see what happens when you deceive people, Rochelle? The pain you inflict on others when you lie?"

Hot tears spilled down her cheeks. "Yes, sir."

"You won't be visiting the post office again, is that clear?"

"Yes, sir."

"I don't like to have to keep training you girls, again and again, but you leave me no choice.

Why will you never learn? Now wipe your tears and go to the cellar."

The words filled her with dread. "No. Please."

He grabbed her arm and roughly shoved her through the cellar door. She heard the click of the lock, the sound of their footsteps walking away, and then the thud of the front door closing behind them. And then she heard nothing at all.

She sank to the steps, cradling her knees against her chest. A sour, musty odor filled her nose and her throat. She would be sick if the training lasted very long. On the dirt floor below, she heard the scuffling and scratching of rats foraging for food. She drew her knees closer to her chest. The scuffling sound grew near, and she closed her eyes tightly against it. In the darkness, a rat scampered across her foot and she cried out.

"Ro Ro?"

Someone gently shook her shoulder, and her eyes flew open. There were deep shadows in the room, but Jace stood beside her bed. The fear on his face rendered her instantly awake. "I'm sorry, Jace. Did I wake you up?"

"It's OK. Did you have a bad dream?"

She was still trembling, soaked with sweat. "Yeah. I guess I did."

"Do you want to wear dad's new jersey?"

"What?"

He held out the black and red football jersey she'd seen earlier. "Dad's jersey. It's for bad dreams. Dad says no monsters will bother you if you wear it. Everybody knows that football players are tough."

"I don't feel very tough right now. Maybe I should wear it."

He handed it to her, and she slipped it on over her pajamas.

"I feel better already."

"I know."

"Do you have bad dreams, too, Jace?"

"Yeah. Sometimes after bad dreams Dad cuddles with me."

"I'm sure that helps."

"Want me to go get him?"

She hid a smile. "No, I think we should let your daddy sleep. He has to work in the morning."

"OK." He gazed at her solemnly. "I could cuddle with you, then."

She moved over, and he climbed in beside her, his warm, soft body snuggled against hers. "Sometimes I have dreams about monsters. Was your dream about monsters?"

"Yes, it was."

"Dad says it helps to talk about it. It makes it not so scary."

She sighed. "I'd rather talk about happy dreams, wouldn't you?"

"Yeah."

"Tell me a happy dream you've had."

He spun an outlandish tale about a land of soda pop rivers, purple horses with pink cotton candy manes, and mountains made of ice cream.

Rochelle smiled in the dark.

"And sometimes if it's a really bad dream dad lets me have graham crackers and milk. Or ice cream."

She stroked his hair. "Your dad's a pretty smart guy."

"Uh-huh. We don't have any ice cream, though."

"No?"

"No. But we have mud pie."

"Do you think a small sliver of mud pie would help?"

"Yes."

"We'll have to be very quiet."

"I know."

They made their way on tiptoe to the kitchen, where Rochelle cut them each a small slice of pie. Their hushed whispers and clinking of silverware must have awakened Sandy because moments later he appeared in the doorway.

"What's going on?" His puzzled glance

rested on the football jersey Rochelle wore.

"Ro Ro had a dream about monsters," Jace told him. "So I gave her the jersey, and cuddled with her, and now we're having just a sliver of pie."

"I see." He moved to the pie, cut a slice, and joined them at the table.

"Can we play Crazy Eights again?"

"Buddy, it's the middle of the night."

"Just one game? Please? To help us get tired again?"

Sandy sighed. "Why not?"

One game turned into two, and two turned into four.

Rochelle popped a bowl of popcorn. As the three of them talked and laughed together into the night, all thoughts of her life in California disappeared, and the monsters seemed a million miles away.

14

The chiming of his cell phone and the sunlight streaming in through the window pulled Sandy from a dead sleep. He sat up, dazed, and reached for his phone. It was after eight o'clock, which left little doubt in his mind as to who was calling. "Hello?"

"Good morning, this is Rita, the secretary at Banner Street Elementary School. May I please speak with Sandy Fairbrother?"

"This is Sandy."

"Hi, Sandy. I'm just calling to find out whether Jace will be coming to school today."

"Yes, he is. I apologize, Rita. We're running a little late this morning, but I'll have him there as soon as I can."

"All right, no problem," she said, though her tone indicated it *was* a problem. "We'll see him shortly, then. Have him come straight to the office and sign in when he gets here."

"Yes, I'll do that." Sandy clicked off the call. He sprang up from the couch, pulled on yesterday's jeans, and hurried upstairs to wake Jace. After coaxing the boy into his school clothes, he gave him a cold toaster pastry and rushed him out the door. They arrived at Jace's school a full forty minutes late. So much for sticking to their routine.

He hurriedly unbuckled Jace's booster seat, and lifted him from the truck. They walked toward to school office together."

"Jace, don't tell anyone about us playing Crazy Eights half the night, all right? It'll be our little secret."

"Why not?"

"Because they'll think your daddy is an idiot."

"OK." Jace grinned and rubbed his knuckles on top of Sandy's head.

Sandy signed and dated the tardy sheet. "I'll pick you up from school and take you to Grandma Sue's for a little while, so I can go to the open house. Have your things together and be ready, OK? No lollygagging around today."

"I won't," the boy promised.

Sandy kissed the beloved mop of curls. "Have a good day, champ. I love you."

"I love you too, Daddy."

Jace disappeared through the student

entrance and Sandy pushed out a breath. What was he thinking, letting his son stay up playing cards half the night on a school night? He'd have to start being more careful about Jace's routine, about keeping the boy's life structured.

Or not.

As he drove away, he couldn't keep from smiling. He finally got it. This was one of those little things Rochelle had talked about. A thousand days and nights would come and go, and Jace would go to bed at a decent hour, and he'd get to school on time the next morning, and those days and nights would be completely forgettable. But last night . . . last night was a night the boy would remember. In a matter of days, Rochelle had come into their lives and turned them upside down. She'd injected a little bit of fun and a whole lot of unpredictability into their ordinary routine. She'd made life a wonderful adventure, and he never wanted it to end. But could he find the courage to tell her?

When Rochelle awoke the house was quiet, and the sun was high in the sky. Groping on the nightstand for her phone, the clock read nearly noon. Goodness, she couldn't remember ever sleeping until noon before.

Not in Bessie's house, and certainly not in the dorm. She lingered in bed for a moment, trying to remember what day it was. Time had become a succession of lovely moments since she'd come to Sandy's house, and with no real routine or pressing commitments, it was a difficult thing to keep track of.

She thought back to last night, or more accurately, early this morning. She had no idea what time it was when Sandy had finally coaxed Jace back to bed, reminding him it was a school night, reminding the boy that they both had a full day ahead of them. *Tuesday.* She pushed back the blankets. The day of Sandy's open house.

Last night's pie plates were still in the sink, along with the popcorn bowl. A deck of Crazy Eights cards lay scattered across the table. The memory of their late-night card game made her smile. It was wonderful being a part of a family again. As she stacked the cards together and put them back in their box, a dark shadow fell across her sunny thoughts. As lovely as the arrangement was, she could not just hang out here indefinitely. Sooner or later, she would have to leave. That was a deep and lonely thought. She didn't want to face what the future would hold, not today.

After a breakfast of cereal and toast, she took stock of Sandy's food inventory. He hadn't been kidding about the abundance of convenience foods, but an investigation of the freezer produced a package of shredded potato rounds, a bag of mixed vegetables, and some frost covered chicken breasts. She would make Bessie's chicken casserole for their dinner. It had been a favorite of hers and Austin's growing up, and Jace would probably love it, too.

Rochelle had done very little cooking during her years in California, but Bessie had taught her and Austin at young ages how to cook, how to run the washing machine, how to keep house, and how to manage a checking account. She wanted them to be able to take care of themselves in life. Skills Ro had never forgotten. As if her thoughts had summoned him, her phone chimed. "Hello, Austin."

"Hey, I've got an update for you."

"I'm listening."

"Our man in California tells me the judge signed a second warrant. They're going through our friend's hotel with a fine-tooth comb today."

She shuddered. "He'll not like that."

"They never do. Are you doing OK out there? Everything quiet?"

"Quiet as a mouse."

"Good. So, we've been keeping a close eye out around town. There haven't been any sightings of the black SUV. And we've left no stone unturned, believe me. It's like the vehicle, and its driver, have vanished into thin air."

"What do you make of that?"

"I think the dude is long gone, Ro. You can probably go back to Bessie's house in a day or two."

Her heart sank. "Is Gus getting to be too much for Kat?"

"No. It's not that. I just thought staying out there might be kind of awkward for you."

The arrangement was anything but awkward, but she wasn't prepared to get into that with Austin. The shadows of dread grew thick around her as she showered, and then tidied the house. She wished she could share Austin's optimism that Menzo's goon had retreated without finding her. But Menzo's people didn't work that way.

The sweet scent of lilacs drifted through the open kitchen window, bringing comforting memories of home. Lilacs had been Bessie's favorite flower, and she'd filled the backyard with lilac trees of white, purple, and palest pink. In the spring she'd cut bouquets for every room in the house. Their colors and scent had brought cheer to even the darkest, rainiest days. It was another of Bessie's little ways of saying *I love you.*

A second search of the cupboards did not produce a single vase, but Rochelle found several empty glass jars in the recycling bin. Armed with an old bushel basket and a pair of scissors, she went outside. A gentle breeze whispered in the trees, and the scent of lilacs mingled with honeysuckle as she strolled down a brick path that was long overtaken by moss. When she reached the crumbling remains of the rock wall, she breathed deeply of the heady spring air. As she cut through the stubborn lilac branches, she thought how lovely it would be to rebuild the wall. Oceans of creeping phlox would cascade down the sides, and she'd plant daisies and bright red cone flowers along the front. But that kind of thinking was futile. This was not her property to landscape. It never would be, and she must not live in her daydreams, as pretty as they were. If Austin believed it was safe for her to return to Bessie's house, then there was no reason for her to stay here any longer.

Back in the kitchen, she'd laid stems of lilacs on the table and was trimming off some of the leaves when she heard the front door open. She froze. Strange, she hadn't heard the truck pull into the driveway. "Sandy?" she called.

When she received no answer, she set down her scissors, wiped her hands on her jeans, and crept to the front hallway. Her disbelieving glance swept over the woman who stood there. As always, she looked like a fashion model, even in faded jeans and matching denim jacket, a white, low-cut shirt setting off her perfect California tan. Her glance moved over the woman's expensive sun-streaked highlights before meeting her exquisite violet eyes.

"Skye?"

"Hello, Rochelle."

Her tone was cool as ice. Any trace of fondness Skye might have felt for her was long gone. A pit of uneasiness lodged in her stomach. "What are you doing here?"

"Thanks for the warm greeting. I was hoping we could talk. Are you alone?"

"I . . . yes."

"Good."

She withdrew her hand from the pocket of her jacket. A small handgun glinted in the sunlight filtering through the open door.

Rochelle's blood rushed to her head as the breath left her lungs.

"Your little disappearing act put me in

very bad place with Menzo," Skye said. "But I'm sure you know that."

"I'm sorry about that, Skye."

"Well, if you're not now, you soon will be."

"You don't have to do this," Rochelle whispered.

Skye laughed. "Oh, but I do. What choice did you leave me?"

Ro's phone chimed in the kitchen. She ignored it.

"How did you find me?"

"We still have your file. All of your personal information was in your application. It didn't take a rocket scientist to figure out you'd come back to Ohio. All I had to do was spend a couple of hours in the local diner, and the rest was easy. You're the talk of the town around here. They seem to think you're some kind of goddess. Except for the old bat who owns the diner. She says you stole her daughter's boyfriend."

She was dizzy. Skye's words tumbled around in her brain, making no sense at all. "What?"

"Sandy Fairbrother? The tall, good-looking contractor who owns this house? The woman says her daughter was practically engaged to him until you showed up. It seems you've gotten very good at taking what's not yours."

"I still have most of the money I took. I'll give you back what I have, and I'll send you the rest, every cent of it. I promise."

"This is not about the money, Rochelle," she hissed. "You made a fool of Menzo, running off like that. That alone would have been enough, but now you've opened your mouth to the wrong people. Now you've become a liability."

"Please listen to me. Together we can put him in jail where he belongs."

Skye's eyebrows shot up. "You can't be serious."

"I am serious. You used to tell me how you dreamed of getting away, of going back to Nebraska and owning a horse farm. Remember? Wide open fields, and clear blue skies, and riding with the wind in your hair. You can do that, Skye. You can be free of him. We both can."

Skye sighed, all at once looking weary. "Maybe you can. But I'm in way too deep for that."

"You were his prisoner. You were brainwashed and exploited just like I was. He coerced you into a life of ugliness, but it's not too late to start over, Skye. Life can still be beautiful."

Skye's expression shifted.

For a moment, Ro thought she'd gotten

through to her. Out in the kitchen, her phone chimed insistently. "Look, that's probably Sandy. If I don't answer it he's bound to come out here looking for me."

In a moment, Skye's expression changed. "Well, he'll be too late, won't he? Now let's go. Bruce is waiting for us at the end of the driveway."

Pushing down her fear, she stood firm. "I'm not going anywhere with you, Skye. You'll have to shoot me."

"Menzo wants you brought back alive. If I go back without you, I'm as good as dead."

"I'm sorry. It won't happen."

"I thought you might feel that way, so I stopped and picked up a little insurance policy on the way."

"What do you mean?"

"We have Jace."

A fist of hard terror gripped her heart. "What?"

"He's unharmed, so far. He was actually quite happy to come with us, to come and see his friend, *Ro Ro.*"

The use of her nickname caused a wave of bile to rush up the back of her throat. This was a complete game changer. They had Jace?

No. Please, God. No.

"Please don't hurt him."

"There won't be a reason to, if you cooperate and don't do anything stupid."

"All right." Her mouth went dry. "I'll go with you. But first you have to let Jace go."

"If you play it smart he won't be harmed. You'll have to take my word for it. Once you're in the SUV, we'll let him go. Now turn around."

As she did so, Skye produced a pair of handcuffs from her jacket and clapped then around Rochelle's wrists. Praying for strength and courage, Rochelle slowly walked out the door, knowing as she did that she was trading her life for Jace's.

At two-thirty, Sandy had left Judge to finish ripping out the old floor at the kitchen reno on Coleson Avenue. He shot over to Banner Street, picked up Jace from school, dropped him at his grandmother's house, and arrived at the open house just ten minutes late. Forty minutes into the open house, Sandy had already spoken with several prospective buyers. He was surprised the woman with the purple eyes had not shown up. She'd seemed genuinely interested in the property.

The nagging feeling he'd had in his gut since leaving Maddy's two nights ago returned. Something about the woman just felt wrong. She claimed to be from Michigan. Football fan or no, he doubted it was possible to live anywhere in Michigan and be unaware of the Michigan-Ohio State rivalry; the greatest sports rivalry in all of North America. Yet she hadn't seemed to catch on to his little joke. Strike one.

She said she'd transferred here for a position at the local hospital. Yet for months, he'd listened to Carol-Anne's endless complaints about her long shifts and reduced pay. The hospital's funds had been woefully mismanaged in the last few years, and according to Carol-Anne, the place teetered on the brink of shutting down. And yet this nurse practitioner had transferred in from out of state? Strike two.

You'll be there the whole time?

He'd foolishly decoded the question as flirtation, but now he was getting the uneasy feeling that the strange woman had wanted to make sure he would be accounted for from three o'clock to six. He could only think of one reason for that.

"I just love the granite countertops," a woman gushed. "And I'm *obsessed* with the wide plank floors! The dark chocolate color is to die for!"

"Above grade laminate?" her husband asked.

"It's actually reclaimed barn wood, one-hundred-percent local," Sandy told him.

"I can see that you didn't cut any corners on the finishes. But what about the wiring and the plumbing?"

"Completely replaced, and up to code."

"New metal roof?"

"Fifty-year guarantee."

"That certainly ought to hold us."

The young couple was almost hooked. He should expound on the house's other selling points, but all at once he felt desperate to hear Rochelle's voice. "Will you folks excuse me for a minute? I have to make a phone call."

Outside, he tried her number. The call went to voicemail. Frustrated, he tried again. Voicemail. After four tries, he placed a second call.

"Hey, Austin. It's Sandy."

"Hey, what's up?"

"I'm not sure. I feel as if something might be going on at the house. I want to check on Rochelle. Can you meet me there in a few minutes?"

"I'm kind of swamped here, Sandy. I just talked to her a couple of hours ago. I'm sure she's fine."

For an entire year, Sandy had disregarded Bessie's concerns about Rochelle because he was sure she was fine. Maybe he was overreacting. They'd had a late night. Maybe when they arrived she would simply be taking a nap, and he'd look like all kinds of a fool. But the strange sense of foreboding told him he'd be an idiot to ignore it.

"I'm not so sure about that, Austin. There was a strange woman in town Sunday night, asking all kinds of questions. I think she might be part of Menzo's network out in California."

"Sunday night? And you're just now telling me?"

"It seemed innocent at the time. But the more I think about it, the less her story adds up."

"OK. I'll grab Joe, and we'll head over there in a couple of minutes."

"Thanks. I'll meet you there."

"If you see anything that seems suspicious, sit tight and wait for us, OK? Don't confront anybody on your own."

"Got it."

He turned the young couple over to Kristin with his apologies and hurried out to his truck. On the way home, he made one last attempt to call Rochelle.

No answer, straight to voicemail.

The short drive from town had never taken so long. Sandy prayed as he sped along the county road, the storm in his stomach growing more turbulent by the minute.

Please let her be all right . . .

He pulled into his driveway, slowing as he bounced along the rutted path. About a quarter of a mile in, he spotted it. Around the second bend, through a break in the trees, the black SUV was parked about two-hundred yards from the house. The sight of it filled him with fury. His first instinct was to race up there, pull the goon from his vehicle, and give him a good throttling.

Wait . . .

It was a Voice Sandy had heard before at the lowest points in his life.

The would-be kidnapper was likely armed, and a rash, impulsive decision on Sandy's part might cost Rochelle her life. He pulled to the edge of the driveway and waited. Moments later Austin's car rolled in behind him.

Sandy got out and approached the car. "The SUV is here, about a quarter of a mile ahead."

Austin blew out a breath. "OK. I guess we'd better get some reinforcements." He called for back-up. He and his partner, Joe Cooper, climbed out of the car. They peered through the trees at the SUV.

"How do you want to play it?" Joe asked.

"Element of surprise," Austin told him. "Sandy, you wait here."

"Not a chance. I'm going with you."

"No, I can't let you do that. This could get real ugly, real fast."

Sandy stood firm. "All due respect, Austin, you can't stop me."

Austin thought for a moment, his jaw muscles working. "All right, but stay down and stand clear of that vehicle."

They scrambled through the trees, trying to be stealthy. Brambles caught Sandy's shirt and branches whipped his face, but he barely noticed. All that mattered was Rochelle, his beautiful Rochelle. His love.

When the SUV was less than fifty feet away, Austin turned to Joe. "I'm moving in. Cover me."

"I got you, brother."

Austin crab-walked to the SUV's passenger side.

The driver peered through window at the path ahead.

Austin bolted upright, his gun drawn. "Get your hands where I can see them," he commanded. "Do it now!"

The man's expression was stunned as he slowly placed both hands on his head.

Joe Cooper moved in.

"He's got a weapon on the seat," Austin

told Joe. To the driver, he said, "We're taking the handgun. Don't do anything stupid."

Joe opened the door and retrieved the weapon.

His own weapon still in hand, Austin moved around to the driver's side. With Joe Cooper covering him, he cuffed the driver's wrist and secured it to the vehicle's grab bar.

"Where is Rochelle?" he demanded.

"She's on her way down from the house."

"Who's with her?"

"My partner, Skye."

"OK, listen very carefully. In a few minutes this place will be crawling with cops, so don't even think about planning an escape. Right now, you're looking at attempted kidnapping. Unless you want to upgrade to attempting to cross state lines with a hostage, you'll do exactly what I tell you to do . . ."

Rochelle stumbled down the driveway ahead of Skye with tears filling her eyes and desperate prayers in her heart. If any harm came to Jace Sandy would never forgive her. She'd never forgive herself. Of course, once Menzo got his hands on her, she wouldn't have long to live with her regrets. He'd kill her, of that, she was sure. And maybe she deserved it.

But Jace was guilty of nothing.

Please, Father God. Let that precious little boy be safe. Please turn this around.

When they rounded the first corner, she saw the SUV sitting on the shoulder of the driveway. As Skye propelled her toward the vehicle, Rochelle peered at the driver through the open window. She recognized him as the man from the plaza. "Where's Jace?" she demanded.

Skye shoved her forward. "You're a fool, Rochelle. You always have been."

Her heart sank as the realization of how skillfully she'd been played dawned. "You don't have him, do you?"

"Nope." Skye smiled smugly. "Never did."

"Any problems?" the man asked.

"My plan worked like a charm, as you can see," Sky said, shoving Ro toward the vehicle. "Now let's get out of here."

The man's murderous glance raked over Rochelle and returned to Skye. He extended his right hand. "Let me have your gun."

"Where's yours?"

"It's here, but it's not firing properly. I did a little target practicing while you were in the house. I think I might have jammed it."

Skye sighed and handed over her weapon.

The man held it for a long moment, his gaze darting to the heavy brush that lined the driveway. And then to Rochelle's utter astonishment, he gently tossed it into the weeds. It landed on the ground with a soft thud.

"What are you doing?" Skye demanded.

"Put your hands on your head, Skye. Do it now!" Austin and Joe stepped out of the trees with their weapons drawn.

"You fool!" Skye shrieked at the man. "You set me up?"

"They already had us," he spat. "So much for your brilliant, well-thought-out plan. They knew we were coming."

"Get down on the ground!" Austin commanded.

Skye sank to her knees. As the handcuffs clicked around her wrists, a police cruiser raced up the driveway, its siren wailing, followed by the county sheriff. Just as Rochelle was sure her legs would give out, Sandy appeared and wrapped her in his arms.

"Ro. Thank God you're safe."

"They said," her voice cracked. "They said they had Jace."

"They don't have him, baby. He's with his grandma, safe and sound."

She sobbed against his chest. "How did you know to come?"

He stroked her hair. "My gut told me you were in trouble. I'm glad I listened to it this time."

In a tangle of confusion, she watched as three officers approached the SUV, retrieved the driver, and put him in the back of a police car.

"Looks like Menzo's tough guy wasn't so tough after all. Let's get you out of those things." Austin approached.

Rochelle turned her back and gratefully extended her wrists.

He slid a key into the lock and within seconds, the cuffs slid off. "Quite an adventure, huh sis?"

"Austin. I'm so glad you came."

"Me, too." He tucked a strand of hair behind her ear, much as Bessie had done when she was small. "The police will want to talk to you. Do you feel strong enough?"

She nodded.

"Just tell them what you told me. Tell them everything, OK? I've got to help take out this trash. Then I have some reports to write. I'll call you later."

"OK."

After embracing her in a fierce hug, he extended his hand to Sandy. "Good work, brother."

Sandy blew out a breath. "You weren't

half bad yourself."

With a grin, Austin turned and walked to the squad car, where Skye and her partner glared from the backseat.

A half hour later, Sandy brewed a pot of coffee.

Rochelle spent the next two hours answering questions and explaining the situation to the police. Finally, the senior investigator, Ted Burns, turned off his recorder and swallowed the last of his coffee.

"It's a mighty good thing Sandy trusted his gut instincts and called Austin. I'd hate to think of the mess you'd be in right now, young lady, if he hadn't. Good work, son."

Sandy waved away the older man's praise. "She's safe now. That's all that matters."

"What will happen to Skye?" Rochelle asked.

"Nothing good, I expect. Kidnapping, labor trafficking, money laundering," he ticked them off on his fingers. "Those are all federal crimes."

"I know it looks bad for her right now, but she was a victim, just like me. He brainwashed her."

"That's something for her attorney to sort out." He stood. "We'll probably want to talk with you again later. For now, get some rest.

You've had a rough day."

When he'd left, Sandy guided Rochelle to the living room.

"I called Sue. She's keeping Jace overnight."

Her eyes filled with tears. "She said they had him. Sandy, I was so afraid."

"That's why you agreed to go with them, isn't it?"

She nodded.

"You planned to sacrifice your own life for my child's. I can't even fathom that, Rochelle. I mean, I would do it, but you barely know my son."

"It was only right. If not for me he would never have been in danger in the first place."

"Even so, it shows what you're made of, what kind of person you really are."

He was looking at her with open admiration. And something else she couldn't name.

"She was so convincing. She even knew about my nickname, Ro Ro."

He sighed. "That's because we met her on Sunday night when we were picking up milkshakes. You know how Jace is. He let the nickname slip, but I thought I'd covered it. I had the nagging feeling that something about her was off after we left Maddy's. I should have mentioned it to Austin right then. I'm sorry I didn't."

"You have nothing to be sorry for. If it wasn't for you I'd probably be halfway to California right now." She shuddered, and he wrapped her in his arms. "I can't stay here any longer, Sandy," she whispered against his chest. "I can't keep putting you and Jace in jeopardy because of the foolish choices I made."

"We've all made foolish choices. But that woman and her pal won't cause us any more trouble. I guarantee it."

"You don't know Menzo. He won't give up so easily. What if he sends someone else? What if he comes here, himself?"

"We'll figure this all out. I promise. For now, you need to get some rest. You look wiped out."

He tucked a blanket around her, and within moments, the day caught up with her and she slept.

She'd let everyone down.

It was the final cheerleading competition of her senior year. The Redford's Crossing Lady Lions were the favorites to win. They'd pulled off every stunt in the competition flawlessly, but in their final performance of the day, Rochelle stumbled and fell during a complicated maneuver, costing her team the prestigious first place trophy. She'd been inconsolable. "I failed, Bessie."

"You didn't fail, child. You did beautifully today."

"I bombed the stunt. I let my whole team down."

Bessie tucked a strand of hair behind Rochelle's ear. *"Your team came in second place out of the whole state. I'd call that pretty good."*

"It's not good enough."

"Not good enough for who, Rochelle? Your coach is very proud of you. And so am I."

"Well, I'm not. I messed up so bad. I could have done better."

"If you could have done better, you would have. You did your best, and that's enough. You are enough. You'll soon learn that life isn't always perfect, my darling girl. But that doesn't mean it can't be wonderful. You have to learn to let yourself be happy. You have to let yourself be loved, mistakes and all . . ."

When the distant chiming of her phone pulled her from her dreams, it was dark outside the windows. The room was bathed in shadows broken only by the soft glow of the kitchen light, and the quiet, broken only by Sandy's murmured words.

"Hey Austin, it's me. No, she's fine. She's sleeping. They what? Are you sure? No kidding. Oh, my goodness . . ." He paused for a moment. "Yes, I'll let her know."

Rochelle crept to the kitchen doorway. Sandy spoke into the phone for a few moments more, then clicked off the call and set her cell phone down on the table. His gaze met hers, his expression unreadable.

"What is it?" she asked. "What's wrong?"

"It's over, Rochelle. Menzo Maricello is dead."

15

"What?" She gripped the door jamb, an expression of stunned disbelief on her face. She looked as if she would faint.

Sandy took her arm and guided her to a chair. "Here, sit down. Let me get you a glass of water." He filled a tall glass from the tap, dropped in two ice cubes, and set it in front of her.

"Are you sure? He's really . . . ?"

"I'm as sure as I can be." He took her hand in his. "You're safe, Ro. Menzo will never hurt you again. Or anyone else."

"It's so hard to believe. What happened?"

"According to Austin's contact, the police raided Menzo's hotel this morning. They found a hidden cache of drugs and illegal weapons, along with more than a dozen underaged girls he was planning to traffic into slavery or prostitution. He tried to deny it, of course, but then the cops discovered one of their undercover agents tied up in a linen closet, beaten and half starved. They also found incriminating documents. Turns out Menzo had been tipped off about the investigation ahead of time. He was making plans to flee the country. He was taking the agent along as a hostage."

"Good heavens!"

"I guess it got pretty volatile after that. Menzo knew he was busted. Rather than surrender peacefully, he threw himself out of a tenth-story window."

She pulled in a jagged breath and let it go. "And they're sure it killed him? He wasn't just injured?"

"He wasn't just injured, Ro. He left the scene in the back of the coroner's wagon. Even Menzo couldn't survive a leap from a tenth-story window."

"He had to be in control, right up to the end," she murmured. "Even if that meant dying."

"He made his own choices, and now you're free to make yours. You're finally free to be who you are."

She sat for a long moment, as if letting that sink in. "I'm not sure I know who that is anymore, Sandy."

He squeezed her hand. "I'm sure it'll take some time before you feel like yourself again, whoever that may be. But you've got the rest of your life to figure it out."

"I guess I can go home, then," she finally said. "Back to Bessie's house, I mean."

Disappointment pooled in his gut. Of course, she would leave now. Why would she stay? "There's no reason you can't. But why don't you stay put for the night. It's getting late."

"What time is it?"

He glanced at the clock. "A little past ten."

"I didn't realize I'd slept so long."

"You had a pretty rough day. When was the last time you ate? You must be starving."

"The breakfast plate you left for me this morning."

Lord, was that just this morning? It seemed like a year had passed since then. He moved to the cupboard and took down two cans of spaghetti, dumped them in a bowl, and popped them in the microwave. When it was heated through, he dished up two plates and set them on the table with a loaf of bread and some butter.

"Not much of a celebration meal for your first day of freedom, but it's the best I can do on such short notice."

She smiled. "It looks pretty good to me."

As they sat together at his table, sharing a simple meal, Sandy's heart overflowed. He wanted this, wanted to keep her here, safe, for always. But now was not the time to tell her so. She did not need another bombshell dropped on her today.

But perhaps a firecracker?

"I have an idea," he said. "Why don't you stay here for just one more day? It will give us a chance to explain things to Jace. I'd hate for him to come home from school tomorrow and have you gone, with no explanation. He might not understand that."

"Of course I will."

"Great. The three of us will have a picnic on the porch tomorrow night, and a proper celebration meal for your new life, anything you want."

"That's easy. A bacon cheeseburger and a strawberry milkshake from Maddy's."

He smiled. "You got it."

The next morning, Rochelle prepared herself a breakfast of eggs, toast, fried potatoes, and bacon. She ate ravenously. The nervous flutter in her tummy was quiet at last. The dark shadow that had fallen across her life was dispelled. She was finally free.

She'd planned to spend her last official day at Sandy's giving the house a top to bottom cleaning, her small way of thanking him for his gracious hospitality. In the back of the hall closet, behind the vacuum cleaner, a cardboard box beckoned to her and she pulled it out. Unfolding the flaps, she saw that it contained the souvenirs of Sandy's life.

Her fingers hovered over the large manila envelope on top labeled Childhood. It would be wrong to look through Sandy's things, a gross invasion of his privacy. But the pull to know him was stronger than her conscience and so she opened the envelope. It contained a thin stack of photos. She removed the first one and studied it. Two towheaded boys stood side by side, their arms around each other's waists. One held a baseball bat and the other wore a catcher's mitt. They were almost identical, except one was taller and slightly older than the other. In a second photo, the boys sat at the top of a Ferris wheel, the smaller boy tucked into the elder's side, the older boy's arm wrapped protectively around his shoulders. On the back, the scribbled words: *Me and Joe, County Fair 1997.* There were two Christmas morning photos of the boys posed in front of a Christmas tree, and one of the boys in winter, sledding down a hill, the younger boy's face alight with happiness, while the older boy's expression was pensive.

She returned the photos to their envelope and reached for a second manila envelope. This one contained Sandy's high school football letters and his diploma. Beneath that was a stack of year books. She lifted out the one on top, their sophomore year. The book fell open to the page where the sophomore class photos were featured. Tucked inside the page, beside her photo, she discovered a corny Valentine of a cartoon dog with the message *"Somebody thinks you're doggone fabulous!"* A red crepe paper rose was stapled to the corner of the card. She turned the card over, and saw her name neatly printed on the back.

Rochelle Delany, Homeroom 3C.

She stared at the card in amazement. The booster club had made the Valentines and sold them to the student body each Valentine's Day, along with the crepe paper roses; silly, ugly things that every girl coveted. Rochelle always received a full bouquet. She fingered the brittle petals of the long-faded rose. Why had she not received this one?

In Sandy's eleventh grade yearbook was another card for Rochelle, this one featuring a kitten. *"Someone thinks you're purrrfect!"* And in his senior yearbook, a third card, a third crepe paper rose. This one said simply, *"Be mine?"* Knowing about the secret valentines made her feel a rush of tenderness for him. She searched her heart, and knew. He had never given her the cards because he had been afraid she would reject them. Reject *him*. But would she have?

At five-thirty, Jace burst through the front door. "Ro Ro! We got hamburgers and milkshakes, and look who else we got!"

Gus plodded into the room behind him.

"Well, hello, old man." She bent to scratch his ears. "Long time, no see. Did you miss me?"

He chuffed and turned away.

"Dad says we're gonna have a picnic out on the porch. We even got a burger for Gus!"

Sandy appeared in the doorway carrying three takeout boxes.

Rochelle raised an eyebrow. "Gus is having a burger?"

He grinned. "What better way to celebrate his homecoming?"

After dinner, the three of them played hide and seek in the yard, and when it grew dark, they went inside.

Jace begged to watch his favorite super hero movie. A half hour into the film he fell asleep with his head in Rochelle's lap.

When the movie ended Sandy gently shook him awake. "Wake up, Champ. It's time for us to take Gus and Ro Ro home."

His expression was crestfallen. "Can't you stay here with us, Ro Ro?"

"Oh, sweetie, I . . ."

"You can sleep in my room. You can sleep in the top bunk. And Gus, too."

She shot a helpless glance at Sandy.

"We talked about this, remember, Buddy?" Sandy said gently.

"That's so nice of you, Jace. I'd love to sleep in the top bunk, and I'm sure Gus would, too. But I have Bessie's house to sleep in."

His arms tightened around her. "I want you to live here with us."

The moment was heartbreaking and beautiful. She dared not look at Sandy again for fear he'd see in her eyes that she understood their losses and that she wanted desperately to be the one who stayed.

"I have to go home and take care of Bessie's house, but I'll tell you what. You can come and see me any time you want to."

"I can?"

"Of course you can. And we'll still spend lots of time together." She stroked his hair. "We'll have picnics and go fishing and play Crazy Eights."

"And hide and seek?"

"And hide and seek."
"And mother may I?"
"Yes, absolutely."
"Tomorrow?"
"We'll see."
"Pinky swear?"
"Pinky swear."

They locked pinkies for a moment, and then Jace reluctantly let her go. He fell back to sleep on the drive to Bessie's house.

She and Sandy made the trip in silence. When they pulled up in front of her temporary home, Sandy lifted Gus from the truck.

"You're sure you'll be all right?" he asked.

"I'll be fine, now that . . . you know."

"Right. But call me if you need anything."

"Thank you, Sandy. For everything."

"It was my pleasure."

"I'll see you soon?"

"You bet."

As she watched them drive away, she thought about forever and how much she would love to spend it with these two precious men.

16

Bessie used to say that life was like a summer sky, filled with both sunshine and clouds. A person had to celebrate the joyful seasons of life and patiently endure the hard ones, knowing that neither season lasts forever. Of all Bessie's words of wisdom, these seemed the most relevant to Rochelle on Saturday morning. In four short days, her entire life had changed. As Sandy had said, she was free now to enjoy this new season, to be who she was. She still wasn't sure exactly what that entailed, but she was looking forward to finding out. One thing was certain. As of six o'clock that morning, she was an auntie.

She pulled into the crowded hospital parking lot and circled the perimeter twice before jamming Bessie's sedan into an empty spot between two other cars. There was no time to be cautious today. Her baby nephew's life had begun, and she didn't want to miss a single moment of it!

In the lobby, she stopped in the hospital gift shop and bought a bouquet of flowers for Kat and a small, plush triceratops for the baby. With a flourish, she signed the card; *With Love from Auntie Ro.* On the envelope, she wrote his name: *Harley Michael Delany.*

She smiled all the way to the maternity ward.

Kat was in the bed, a small bundle cradled against her chest. Austin sat in a chair beside her. They both looked radiant, if exhausted.

"Hello, Auntie," Kat said.

Rochelle crept toward her, happy anticipation swirling.

As Kat unwrapped the bundle, the baby's eyes opened and fixed on her.

Ro's heart overflowed with love. Even at just hours old, Harley was the picture of Austin, except for a shock of downy red hair on his head. "Well hello there, handsome," she cooed. "Where'd you get all that red hair, huh?"

"From his beautiful Irish mama," Austin said.

"Would you like to hold him?" Kat asked.

The invitation stole her breath. "I'd love to."

Austin moved from the chair and after Ro was settled, he gathered up the baby and gently placed him in her waiting arms.

Harley Michael.

Her brother's son. As Ro traced her fingers gently over his perfect hands and his downy cheeks, the wonder of him left her speechless. A tiny, sweet smelling bundle of hope, the baby represented all that was right and beautiful in the world. "Oh, my goodness," she said in a soft tone. "Look at you."

"He's perfect, isn't he?" Kat beamed.

"Yes, he is. Absolutely perfect in every way." She gently touched a tiny ear. "When you get a little bit bigger, Auntie Ro has a lot of plans for you, Harley Michael. We'll go swimming and bike riding at the park. We'll go to the zoo and the aquarium. Auntie Ro will teach you the names of all of the stars."

"And Daddy will take you to basketball games and teach you how to dribble and shoot," Austin said, peering over her shoulder.

"And Mommy is planning the most amazing birthday parties for you," Kat added. "And we'll build snowmen in the winter, and in the fall we'll carve pumpkins. We'll have a beautiful life, little man."

All too soon, a nurse appeared in the

room. "It's a little past time for this guy's feeding," she said. "Would you like some help with nursing him again?"

"I wouldn't turn it down," Kat confessed.

"You'd probably like some privacy." Rochelle reluctantly handed her nephew to the nurse. "I didn't realize it was getting so late, anyway. I should probably go."

Austin stood, planted a kiss on his son's forehead and then one on Kat's. "I'm going to the cafeteria to grab a cup of coffee. I'll walk Ro to the lobby."

They took the elevator down in silence. When they reached the first floor, Rochelle asked, "When do you think Kat and the baby will be released to go home?"

"We're hoping for tomorrow."

"Will Kat need any help with the baby? I mean, I know I'm no childcare expert, but I'll be happy to come and hold him if she wants to take a nap or anything."

"Her mother's staying with us for a few days, until we get the hang of things."

"Even so, call me if you guys need anything. Day or night, OK?"

"OK."

"He's incredible, Austin. I'm so happy for you both. And for myself, too."

"Thanks." As she turned to leave, he said softly, "Ro?"

She turned back.

"I'm glad you're here."

She smiled. "Me, too."

"Listen, I'm sorry, about the way I acted when you first got home. I was a real jerk."

She waved the apology away. "It's OK."

"No, it's not OK. There's no excuse for it, I just . . ." He sighed. "I won't lie to you. It tore me apart when you left. I felt like I'd lost my best friend. Then when you didn't stay in touch, I felt like I'd been abandoned again. I couldn't get past my own anger and hurt to see that you might be hurting, too." He blinked back tears. The confession was difficult for him.

"I'm sorry, too, Austin," she said, as tears seeped from her eyes. "For all of it."

"You have nothing to be sorry for. Sandy feels guilty that he didn't take Bessie's concerns seriously. But Ro, she expressed those concerns to me, too, and I didn't act on them. Sandy was just a family friend, but I was your brother. It was my job to look out for you. I'm sorry I let you down."

She wrapped him in a hug. "You never let me down."

"I sure feel like I did." He pulled away and looked into her eyes. In a sing-song voice he chanted softly, "Clover, clover, can I do it over?"

The memory was bittersweet, and it made her smile. She'd invented the game of clovers, a variation of hopscotch, to amuse him in the frightening days after their parents took off. She and Austin had spent countless summer evenings playing it on the broken concrete of their patio. Again and again, Austin would lose his balance while hopping from one to the other of the chalk clovers she'd drawn. Again and again, he begged for a do-over.

"I wish we could both go back and do things differently," she said. "But we can't."

"Let's go forward, then. Together."

She smiled. "I'd really like that."

"I love you, sis."

"I love you, too. So much."

Rochelle left the hospital feeling as if a hundred-pound weight had been lifted from her shoulders. After years of rain, maybe her season in the sun had finally arrived. Maybe it took leaving to make her understand how wonderful it was to come home, to make her find out that the things she'd walked away from were precious. Now that the realization had dawned, she intended to grab hold of those precious things and never let go.

Starting with Sandy Fairbrother.

She'd play it cool. Even so, she was barely

in the front door of Bessie's house when she called him. "I've got some news."

"Good news, I hope?"

"The best. As of six o'clock this morning I'm an auntie."

"No kidding? Hey, congratulations. Boy, right?"

"Yes, a beautiful baby boy. Harley Michael. Eight pounds and three ounces."

"Ooh, a bruiser."

She laughed. "Yep."

"I'll have to get started showing him some of my famous football plays soon."

"Yep, just as soon as Austin finishes teaching him how to shoot baskets."

"And how are Harley's mom and dad doing?"

"They're on top of the world, as you can imagine. Kat might be getting released from the hospital tomorrow, which is part of the reason I'm calling. Would you be free to take the cradle over to their house with me this evening? I'd like for it to be there waiting for them when Kat and the baby arrive home."

He laughed softly. "Do great minds think alike, or what? I planned to call you later and ask you the same question. Do you want to grab something to eat, afterwards?"

"Sure."

"I'll be tied up at the open house until at least four o'clock. How about I come by for you at six?"

"I'll see you then." Smiling, she disconnected the call.

She went to her closet and pulled out the two dresses she'd bought at the plaza the week before. Gus plodded into the room. "I'm glad you're here, Gus, I need a second opinion. What do you think? Do you like the red one better, or the pink one?"

Gus stared at her for a long moment before turning away.

"Are you still mad at me?"

He chuffed and stared at the wall.

"Don't try to play the victim with me, Gus. I know for a fact that Kat spoiled you rotten while you were there." She sank to her knees beside him and stroked his head. "Remember when I said your new master was a piece of work? Turns out I was wrong. So much has changed for me in the last few days. I still don't know exactly who I am, but I know what I want. Now I just have to figure out how to get it."

At four o'clock Sandy left the open house on Sullivan Street. It had been a positive showing, with two solid offers written that day. Things were looking up.

He knew about the baby before Rochelle called him. Austin had called with the news hours before, and had asked if Sandy could have the cradle at the house tomorrow, when Kat and the baby arrived home. Sandy had put his plan in motion after Austin's call. Rochelle had merely saved him a step.

From the open house, he stopped at Sue's and let her know the plan was a go, and then he explained it all to Jace. He drove home to shower and change his clothes, taking extra care to tame his unruly cowlick with a dab of styling gel. With an hour to kill, he found himself pacing from room to room, his nerves stretched tight. Jace had been over the moon with his idea, as Sandy had known he would be. Sandy would never in a million years have chanced setting his son up for rejection.

But he'd seen something in Rochelle's eyes the night he gave her the news about Menzo. He'd seen it again the following night, when Jace begged her to stay with them. A deep, soul longing that matched his own. Less than a week ago he'd come close to losing her forever. Knowing that had sobered him, had emboldened him to take action. Plucking up his courage, he'd gone to the jewelers in the plaza and bought an engagement ring, a small diamond solitaire in a gold setting. Then, he started planning the perfect way to surprise her with it. As he took the ring from its hiding place in his dresser and slipped it in his pocket, he hoped he hadn't made a terrible mistake.

He wandered to the kitchen and poured a glass of water. It had been three days since Rochelle returned home to Bessie's house. And though she'd only been with him and Jace for four days, the house seemed unbearably empty without her. Cold and dark, as if the sun had hidden behind a cloud. But if his plan worked out, the sun would soon be shining again.

Please, God, he prayed, as he fingered the small, black velvet box in his pocket. *Either way. Please help me to accept Your will.*

When he arrived at Bessie's house an hour later, Rochelle met him on the porch, looking incredible in a pink summer dress, her hair a dark, glossy dream hanging down her back. She'd put on lipstick, accentuating her full, tantalizing lips. With one look at her, he knew that a simple friendship would never be enough. He loved this woman. He'd loved her for half of his life and it was high time he told her so. "You look beautiful," he said.

"Thank you. You don't look half bad, yourself. Are you ready?"

He pulled in a breath, his nerves screaming. Yes, he was ready. He'd never been more ready for anything in his life.

They drove across town to Austin's house and Rochelle unlocked the front door.

Sandy deposited the cradle in the nursery upstairs.

Rochelle had brought a roll of purple and green ribbon. She tied it into an elaborate bow and laid it in the cradle. "What does Austin owe you for this?" she asked. "I want to buy it for Harley as a baby gift from Auntie Ro."

"Too late. It's already a gift from Uncle Sandy."

She grinned at him. "Are you sure?"

"Absolutely, positively."

"You're a good man, Uncle Sandy," she said.

Good enough to marry? He held her gaze for a long moment before looking away.

Back in the truck, he was rethinking his earlier idea of picking up burgers and eating them in the park. With Rochelle looking all glamorous in her pink dress and makeup, that plan seemed all wrong now. What he had in mind required candlelight, soft music, and vases of long-stemmed roses on linen-covered tables. How could he have been so moronic? He should make a Plan B. He should shoot Sue a text and tell her the plan had changed.

"Is the Top of the Town still in business?" Rochelle asked, causing him to shift gears once again.

"It's changed hands. It's called Jerry's now, but yeah, it's still open."

"Do they still make those amazing barbeque beef sandwiches?"

"I'm pretty sure they do."

"Bessie used to take us there sometimes on Saturday nights. I've been craving one of those sandwiches ever since I got back to town."

"Jerry's it is, then." He started up the truck and pulled from the curb. Back to Plan A.

When they arrived at Jerry's the parking lot was packed with cars.

"Can we order them to go?" she asked. "I don't feel like playing Twenty Questions with half the town tonight."

"I understand."

He went inside and ordered the sandwiches, along with drinks and two orders of Jerry's famous potato wedges. He shot Sue a quick text.

All is on schedule.

Sandy headed back to the truck.

"It's a pretty night. Would you like to sit in the park?" he asked.

"Sure."

He drove to Main Street Park and they carried their food to the gazebo. Over dinner, she talked animatedly about Bessie's stained-glass ornaments and her plans to create a memorial tree at Christmas in Bessie's honor.

"I think she would have loved that." His heart thudded against his ribs. "Sounds as if you're planning to stay in Redford's Crossing, then?"

"You couldn't tear me away. Not with that beautiful baby boy to help raise."

Their talk turned to baby Harley and Rochelle's eyes sparkled as she talked about the future she envisioned as his aunt.

"He's absolutely perfect, Sandy. His little fingers, his nose. A baby is such a miracle."

"One of God's finest," he agreed. Steeling himself, he blurted, "I'd like to have another one . . . or more someday."

She smiled. "Me, too."

His heart leapt. "Really?"

"Does that surprise you?"

"A little bit. I guess I thought of you as more of a career woman."

"Women can be both, Sandy."

"Oh, I know."

She finished her sandwich and wiped her hands on a napkin. "As I said before, I still don't know what I want to be when I grow up."

"Well, if it turns out you want to hang drywall, I can always use the help."

"I'll keep that in mind."

They laughed together for a moment, and she said, "I never asked you how your open house went today."

"It was a good turnout. In fact I'm pretty sure I've got the house sold."

"Sandy, that's wonderful. Congratulations."

"Thanks."

"So what's next? I see that spooky old house on Bennett Avenue is up for auction. The one everybody always said was haunted. That could be your next great challenge."

He winced. "I'm not feeling anywhere near that ambitious. I've actually been thinking that after we wrap up the kitchen remodel we're doing, I might put some work into my own place."

She bit into a potato wedge. "What are you thinking of doing with your house?"

"Maybe I'll do a kitchen remodel of my own, make it more user friendly. In case anyone wants to come by and make us another pie."

She grinned, melting his heart. "Ahh, so there's a method to your madness."

"I won't lie. I kind of liked having you there." He added softly, "I kind of loved it."

"I kind of loved it, too."

He raised his gaze to meet hers, his heart pounding. "You did?"

"Yeah."

"Maybe . . ."

"Maybe, what?"

His gaze moved over her, taking in her eyes, her lips, her hair. He thought of the beautiful heart that was contained within her external loveliness. She was everything he wanted, everything he'd ever wanted. He hadn't dared to tell her, as a shy sixteen-year-old kid. But now the time had come. *Where was Jace?*

"Back in high school I always wanted you to wear my ring. But I never dared to ask you."

"Are you serious?"

"Yes, I'm serious. You didn't even know I was alive."

"I'm sorry."

"It's my own fault. I didn't have the nerve to talk to you, let alone ask you out on a date. But now that we're older, wiser, I wonder if . . ." He was stumbling, fumbling, failing badly. His glance darted to the parking lot. *Where was Jace?*

"Sandy Fairbrother, are you asking me to go steady?"

He laughed. "Well, we could start there, sure."

"And where would we end?" Her tone was light, but her eyes seemed to pierce the depths of his soul.

His mouth went dry. The ring suddenly felt like a boulder in his pocket.

Sue's white minivan drove into the park. It circled around the lot and headed slowly toward the gazebo, finally pulling into an empty parking spot. Sue opened the side door, and then Jace climbed out of the van.

Rochelle followed his gaze.

"Ro Ro!" Jace ran toward them, a dozen red balloons in the shapes of hearts bobbing behind him as he clutched their strings in his hand.

"What is this?" Rochelle asked.

"Jace has something he wants to ask you." It wasn't the most romantic proposal in the world. Sandy knew that. But he also knew it was exactly the right proposal. He had to make it clear from the start that he and Jace were a package deal.

Jace reached them then, his cheeks ruddy

and his eyes shining. He thrust the bouquet of balloons at Rochelle. "Surprise!"

"Well, thank you, Jace. This is a surprise. What beautiful red balloons." Her questioning gaze moved to Sandy.

"Me and Gramma bought them at the dollar store, but dad gave us the money, and the line was a mile long, and we didn't want to be late, 'cause we're gonna pop the question!"

Her expression changed and became unreadable. "What question is that, Jace?"

He looked at Sandy and Sandy nodded.

"The question is will you *marry* us?" he shouted.

Sandy could no longer hear the birds chirping in the trees, or the children playing tag across the park. He could hear nothing but the question hanging in the air and his own pulse roaring in his ears. He barely dared to breathe as Rochelle dropped to a squat and took his son's face into her hands.

"Getting married is serious business, you know that, right?"

Jace nodded solemnly. "Yes."

"I'd be coming to live in your house forever. You'd have to teach me how to dig up night crawlers in the morning, and help me make chocolate pies. And you'd have to share your daddy with me."

"I don't mind."

"So you're sure you can do all that?"

Jace started bobbing up and down. "Yes. I can do it. Will you marry us, Ro Ro?"

"Sweetie, I thought you'd never ask." She placed a kiss on his forehead, smiling through tears.

Sandy couldn't see her through the tears that brimmed in his own eyes, could not be certain he'd even heard her correctly.

As Jace jumped up and down, the balloons escaped his grasp.

Rochelle moved around the table.

Sandy took her hand in his and slid the ring on her finger. She gasped softly, and then, as a dozen red balloons drifted toward the heavens, every dream he'd ever dreamed came true.

Rochelle Delany kissed him, Sandy Fairbrother, on purpose.

17

Rochelle and Sandy had spent the entire summer rebuilding the rock wall. They'd made what seemed like a hundred trips on their Saturday morning excursions to the creek bed outside of town, and she, Sandy, and Jace had hand-picked each rock and brought them home by the truckload. There were oblong and rectangular rocks, round and square, and even some in the shape of hearts. Stone upon stone, they'd set them in the wall, each layer mortared together to withstand the merciless Midwestern windstorms. They wanted the wall to last forever, like their love.

In the evenings, around the fire pit, they toasted marshmallows and sang songs and told stories, and Rochelle knew they were not merely building a wall. They were building a life.

When the project was finished, she paid a visit to Meg Levy at Blooms Galore, which had been Bessie's favorite nursery. She told Meg her ideas for the rock garden and asked her for suggestions. Meg came out the next day armed with pots of bold, white daisies, fiery red cosmos, and dainty miniature delphiniums, as blue as the summer sky. With each new flower they set into the earth, the garden came more alive. It was gorgeous beyond Rochelle's dreams.

"Thank you so much, Meg," she said.

"It's my pleasure, honey," the older woman assured her. "Consider it my wedding gift to you and Sandy. And my last gift to Bessie. She would love that you're doing this, building this garden."

"Do you think so?"

"Child, I can feel her here, smiling down on us right now." She tapped her heart. "Can't you?"

And with the sunshine glinting off the pond and birdsong filling the air, Rochelle had to admit that she could.

For two weeks in August, she'd been banished from the backyard while Sandy worked on a surprise wedding gift of his own. Finally one evening Jace called her, his voice bubbling with excitement.

"Ro Ro, can you come over tonight and bring marshmallows? We're gonna have a bonfire and make s'mores after you see your surprise!"

"You mean I can finally go out back and see what you two have been up to all this time?"

Jace giggled. "Yep."

When she arrived at the house that evening, they blindfolded her. Sandy took one hand, and Jace the other, and they walked her to the rock wall, Jace impatiently pulling her along.

"Slow down, Champ," Sandy cautioned. "We don't want her to fall."

"I know. But she's gonna be so happy, aren't you, Ro Ro?"

Rochelle smiled. "If you're happy, I'll be happy."

When they stopped walking, Sandy removed the blindfold.

Rochelle's breath caught and her eyes filled with tears.

Jace jumped up and down, still holding her hand. "Surprise! We made you a little house!"

The gazebo sat between the rock wall and the pond, a white octagonal structure with gingerbread trim and built-in benches. Sandy had strung it with white fairy lights, and it glowed softly in the evening shadows.

"You made this for me?" she asked, incredulous.

"I wanted my beautiful girl to have a beautiful space to call her own."

"Dad says you can come out here sometimes if we start to drive you crazy," Jace told her. "We even brought out some magazines and a special mug for your coffee. You can drink it out here without all the commotion so you don't have to be grumpy in the mornings. Come and see!"

As she followed him inside, the tears she'd been holding back suddenly flowed down her face. She did not deserve this man, this child, this gazebo, this life . . .

"Don't you like it, Ro Ro?" Jace asked, a worried expression on his face.

She knelt and kissed his forehead. "I love it so much. And I love both of you for building it for me."

Their plans, their life, had all come together like a dream. As she surveyed the scene before her this September day, Rochelle wept again for the sheer joy of it. The rock wall stretched out before her, stunning in the afternoon sunshine.

Her wedding day. At last.

"Oh, sweetie, I know. It's a crazy, happy, beautiful day." Kat pulled her close for a hug. "But here, don't ruin your make up." She handed Rochelle a tissue and Rochelle dabbed the happy tears from her eyes.

Sandy had built flower boxes on each side of the gazebo, and on this glorious morning, they overflowed with pink and white sweetheart roses and baby's breath. A matching garland festooned the gazebo's eight sides. Rows of folding chairs were set up in front, each one occupied. They'd initially planned a small affair, but as Sandy said, when you'd lived in a town your whole life and knew everyone, where did you draw the line?

She looked at the people in attendance, her town — her friends.

Vanessa Green, who chaired Redford's Crossing's homelessness committee. At Sandy's suggestion, Rochelle had contacted Vanessa about offering free haircuts at the homeless shelter two days a month. A gentle soul who'd also seen her share of hard times, Vanessa had quickly become one of Ro's favorite people.

Bella Thorndike, Bessie's oldest and dearest friend, who owned the local quilt shop. Bella had insisted on making Rochelle's wedding dress, an elaborate mass of pearls and lace that hugged her body like a mother's arms.

Roy Peters from the computer shop, Sandy's high school buddy who'd rigged up lights and speakers for the day's event.

Their friends from church, who'd spent the entire day before, setting up and decorating tables for the reception.

Maddy Sheridan and her daughter, Carol-Anne, who'd finally forgiven Sandy and Ro for falling in love after Carol-Anne had fallen in love with Judge Forrester, Sandy's right-hand man.

In a few short weeks, these people she'd once thought of as dull and narrow-minded had become her mothers, her sisters, her aunts, her uncles, and her cousins, the extended family she'd never had. She thanked God for every one of them.

The music stopped and Jace turned to her. "Is it now, Ro Ro?"

She drew a breath. "Yes, sweetie, it's now."

With a wide grin, he set off down the path, carefully balancing the rings on the red velvet pillow that Kat had made and he had decorated with garish beads and gaudy rickrack. Rochelle had never seen anything more beautiful. After a few steps, he turned and hurried back to give her a spontaneous hug. "I love you, Ro Ro."

"I love you too, Jace. With all my heart."

"Let's go, baby. Everyone's waiting," Kat told him. With a squeeze of Rochelle's hand, she turned and followed Jace down the path, her pale peach gown and auburn hair blazing beneath the brilliant autumn sun.

"Are you ready for this, sis?" Austin asked.

She nodded. "Ready or not, here I come."

"I wish Bessie was here to see this."

"She is." Rochelle knew in her heart that it was true. As she touched the diamond pendant that rested against her heart, she had never felt Bessie's presence more strongly than today.

Austin tucked her arm in the crook of his elbow and as the wedding march played, they made their way to the gazebo.

Sandy stood tall and handsome in his gray tuxedo. Like his son, he couldn't seem to keep a grin from spreading across his face as she moved toward him and her heart overflowed. Sandy. Her partner. Her love.

She heard again the echo of Bessie's words.

You'll find, my darling girl, that sometimes, God's most glorious answers are to the prayers you never even prayed. He loves us enough to give us what we didn't know we wanted.

God's love was tangible today, filling the air around her. And in the moment she took Sandy's hand, deep in her heart, she felt Bessie smile.

Bessie, the woman to whom she owed so

much. The woman who'd taught her to love God, and to love herself. The woman whose prayers had brought her home.

Epilogue

One year later

It had taken nearly a year for Skye Song's case to go to trial. When Rochelle was called to testify for the defense on Skye's behalf, she knew it was the right thing to do. Even so, it was the most difficult thing she'd ever been asked to do in her life.

It was more painful than she'd ever imagined it would be, exposing her dark secrets to a courtroom full of strangers. But the story of the abuse that she and Skye, along with so many other young girls, had suffered under Menzo's control, was one that needed to be told. Sandy's presence in the courtroom had given her the strength to get through it. And to speak with the reporters afterward. There were so many monsters like Menzo still out there, still destroying innocent lives, and Rochelle knew she had to do all that was in her power to save them.

She'd told the jury about a different Skye

than the one who sat before them, a fresh-faced girl of seventeen who'd answered Menzo's advertisement; a minister's daughter, a runaway from a small Nebraska town. Alone on the streets for the first time in her life, Skye had been vulnerable to Menzo's promises and his lies. He'd provided her with security, and then used it as a weapon against her. He'd pulled her into his dark world of prostitution and illegal drugs. She'd survived by making herself indispensable to him. Although her crimes carried a maximum punishment of twelve years in prison, the judge had taken all of the factors into consideration and Skye's sentence had been commuted to a drug and alcohol rehab facility where Rochelle hoped she would get the help she needed. In the end, Rochelle felt that she, too, was at last, truly free.

As ugly as Rochelle's decade-long nightmare in California had been, some good had come out of it. The experience had awakened a deep feeling of compassion inside her and a sincere desire to help other women who had been brutalized.

Sandy had restored Bessie's beloved home to a thing of beauty, just as Bessie had asked him to. Together, he and Rochelle had quietly gifted the property to Rachel's

Hope, a private agency that provided services for victims of domestic abuse. *Bessie's House* was now in use as a safe house for battered women and runaways.

The day after the trial ended, she and Sandy walked hand in hand along the canopied paths in the redwood forest. It was strikingly beautiful and supremely spiritual, strolling together in the hushed shadows of the centuries-old trees.

They stopped beside the massive trunk of a two-hundred-year-old redwood, and Sandy asked a tourist to take their picture. Later, when they sat to rest on a bench beside a chortling creek, he reviewed the photo on his phone.

"I'll print this one out," he said. "Maybe I'll even have it framed and hang it on the wall in my office."

"It will be a nice memento of the trip," she agreed.

"It's more than that, Ro. This photo, this day, represents two answered prayers, two dreams of mine that finally came true."

"Two?" she asked softly.

"I got to walk through the redwood forest, and I got to marry you." He took her hand in his, raised it to his lips, and kissed it. "That's two huge items off my bucket list. If I never accomplish another thing, those two will be enough."

She smiled, knowing that the day would be significant for another reason, as well. That in years to come Sandy would look at the photo and remember this moment as one of the best moments of his life. She'd been waiting for the right moment to tell him, and everything inside her told her that the moment had arrived.

"Three items," she said softly.

"What's the third one?"

"We're going to have a baby."

He stared at her for a long moment as the words slowly sank in.

"What?"

"We're going to have a baby, Sandy."

"Are you sure?"

"Yes. I'm sure. I saw Dr. Patterson last week."

He grinned. And then he folded her into his arms and held her and she felt his warm tears against her skin.

"Are you OK?" she asked.

"I'm more than OK, babe. I'm just about the happiest man in the world right now." He pulled away and gazed into her eyes. "I love you more than life, Rochelle Fairbrother. Did I ever tell you that?"

"Mmm, maybe once or twice. But don't ever stop."

"Not a chance." His hands gently cupped her still flat stomach, no evidence of the miracle growing inside. "I love you so much."

She rested her head on his shoulder as the words escaped into the atmosphere and became a part of the air and the creek and the trees. She breathed in the sheer loveliness of the moment, knowing that no moment in her life ever had or ever would be more true or sacred or beautiful.

The following day, Rochelle left California for the last time. She and Sandy spent much of the five-hour flight dreaming together about their child.

"Jace will be so excited when he finds out he's going to be a big brother," Sandy said.

"I can't even imagine."

"How should we give him the news?"

"I was thinking you could take him to play in the park. I'll meet you both there with a ginormous bouquet of pink and blue balloons."

He smiled. "Perfect."

As the plane entered the airspace above Ohio, they fell silent, gazing in wonder at the mountains and valleys below. The autumn trees that blanketed the rolling Appalachian foothills gleamed like gold, looking like a little bit of heaven on earth.

Rochelle and Sandy held hands, silent, enjoying the view, as the plane soared across the endless blue skies, carrying them home.

A DEVOTIONAL MOMENT

If we confess our sins, he is faithful and just and will forgive us our sins and purify us from all unrighteousness.
~ 1 John 1:9

Falling away from God can happen even to the strongest Christian. They succumb to worldly fears, sometimes caught in a trap of things beyond their control, with no way out . . . or so it seems. But God is with us even in the dark times. All we have to do is surrender our shortcomings and ask for forgiveness and restoration.

In *The Little Things,* the protagonist is caught in a web of deceit that she unknowingly stepped into as a teen. Sin heaps upon sin, until one day, she escapes. But terror stalks her, and as she becomes involved in the fragile struggle for a better life, old fears return to haunt her new beginning. Terrified, she confesses her sins to her family, and to God.

Have you ever been so frightened or ashamed of your past choices that you didn't think you could find your way back? It's true that sometimes, even when you know you're forgiven, you're so afraid to lose it that you can't even rejoice that God saved you. When you feel that way, and you know you've repented and received forgiveness, it's important to acknowledge aloud that you know you're forgiven. It is a trick of the enemy to keep you feeling ashamed and scared. Don't let that happen to you. Allow God's peace to descend. Because you're forgiven, no matter what your emotions tell you, your hope and future are bright. God has forgiven you, so take a giant step forward . . . and forgive yourself.

LORD, HELP ME TO MAKE THE RIGHT CHOICES AND IF I FAIL, SHOW ME THE WAY BACK TO YOU. IN JESUS' NAME I PRAY, AMEN.

ABOUT THE AUTHOR

Changing seasons. Unexpected blessings. Love that lasts forever. These are a few of **M. Jean Pike's** favorite things. With a writing career that has spanned two decades, Jean combines an insatiable curiosity about humans and why they do what they do with a keen interest in the in the quirky and offbeat things in life to bring readers unforgettable tales of life, love, and the inner workings of the human heart. Her short works have been featured in *Chicken Soup for the Soul* and the *Lutheran Digest.*

The employees of Thorndike Press hope you have enjoyed this Large Print book. All our Thorndike Large Print titles are designed for easy reading, and all our books are made to last. Other Thorndike Press Large Print books are available at your library, through selected bookstores, or directly from us.

For information about titles, please call:
(800) 223-1244

or visit our website at:
gale.com/thorndike